"You might want to get somebody over to Miranda's house to fingerprint the windows," Jenna said.

"Why?"

"I think somebody came to visit while I was there today."

"What?" He looked at her in alarm.

As she explained what had happened, a new uneasiness swept through Matt. Had the killer returned to the scene of the crime?

"I just got the sensation that I wasn't alone in the house, but it may have been my imagination working overtime." She picked up her water glass and took a sip.

"Do you suffer from an overactive imagination normally?" he asked.

She smiled wryly. "Never."

Matt frowned and stared at her. "Both of the victims were brunettes with blue eyes—just like you."

CARLA CASSIDY

SCENE *of the* CRIME:
BRIDGEWATER, TEXAS

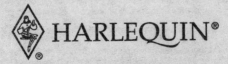

TORONTO • NEW YORK • LONDON
AMSTERDAM • PARIS • SYDNEY • HAMBURG
STOCKHOLM • ATHENS • TOKYO • MILAN • MADRID
PRAGUE • WARSAW • BUDAPEST • AUCKLAND

Recycling programs
for this product may
not exist in your area.

ISBN-13: 978-0-373-69442-6

SCENE OF THE CRIME: BRIDGEWATER, TEXAS

www.eHarlequin.com

Printed in U.S.A.

ABOUT THE AUTHOR

Carla Cassidy is an award-winning author who has written more than fifty novels for Harlequin Books. In 1995, she won Best Silhouette Romance from *RT Book Reviews* for *Anything for Danny*. In 1998, she also won a Career Achievement Award for Best Innovative Series from *RT Book Reviews*.

Carla believes the only thing better than curling up with a good book to read is sitting down at the computer with a good story to write. She's looking forward to writing many more books and bringing hours of pleasure to readers.

Books by Carla Cassidy

CAST OF CHARACTERS

Jenna Taylor—The FBI agent wants to solve her best friend's murder but instead finds herself the next target.

Sheriff Matt Buchanan—A killer walks his streets. Is he smart enough to save the women who live in his town and the beautiful FBI agent who is under his skin?

Miranda Harris—The first victim of a serial killer.

Carolyn Cox—The second victim of a serial killer.

Leroy Banks—Did the busboy hide a killing rage?

Dr. Patrick Harris—The town's veterinarian and a man with a secret past. Would he kill to keep his secrets?

Bud Carlson—Did Miranda reject his bad-boy advances, and did that rejection result in her murder?

Chapter One

Special Agent Jenna Taylor looked up the quiet residential street, then down the other way. Seeing nobody around, she carefully pulled aside the crime scene tape that was stretched across the front door of the small ranch house.

It was wrong, she knew what she was doing was wrong, but she didn't intend to touch anything, wouldn't do anything to compromise the crime scene.

She was surprised to find the door unlocked. She frowned, marveling at the sloppy work of whoever was in charge.

The faint smell of death lingered in the foyer even though she knew the body of the victim had been removed forty-eight hours earlier.

The first thing she saw as she stepped into the foyer was the horrendous painting of a rustic old red barn with a pond in front of it.

The sight of it threatened to unravel the tight control

she'd kept on her emotions since she'd heard about the murder.

She'd painted the picture years ago in the very first art class she'd taken. It held all the flaws of an amateur; the water was too blue, the trees a single shade of green. Jenna had been going to trash it, but Miranda had insisted she loved it and wanted to keep it.

Over the years it had become a running joke between them. No matter where Miranda moved, no matter what her circumstances, the painting was always the one thing constant in her life.

Jenna steeled herself as she stepped into the living room. The essence of Miranda filled the room, from the colorful throw pillows on the red sofa to the plethora of flourishing plants in front of the windows.

Miranda had loved color and life. She made friends easily and trusted in the goodness of people. She and Jenna had been polar opposites, and yet they had been as close as blood sisters.

Jenna had been told very little about the crime, only that Miranda had been murdered and her body had been found in the bedroom. Jenna hadn't spoken to any of the local officials yet. She'd wanted to come here first, see the scene without anyone tainting her first impressions, without anyone giving her theories about the killer. It was how she worked best—completely alone.

She'd been surprised that there hadn't been a patrol

car out front, a guard to keep looky-loos away. That, coupled with the unlocked front door made her slightly ill. The local law in this po-dunk Texas town probably didn't know the first thing about conducting a murder investigation.

It didn't matter. Jenna would see to it that the guilty party was brought to justice. That was her job and she was damn good at what she did.

As she moved down the hallway toward the master bedroom, she reached for the cool emotional detachment that had served her well all of her life. She didn't think about the murdered woman being Miranda.

It was a victim, nothing more. It was the only way she could do her job effectively.

Still her stomach clenched as she reached the door to the master bedroom. It was closed and for a moment she stood before it and drew a couple of deep, slow breaths.

The doorknob was cool beneath her fingers as she turned it and pushed open the door. Evening shadows were already filling the room and although she would have liked to turn on the light, she fought the impulse, not wanting to draw attention to her presence here.

The king-size bed stood before her. It had been stripped of sheets and blankets and only an ugly rust-colored stain remained in the center of the mattress.

This was where Miranda had died. She'd come to this town to begin to build a new life and instead had been killed in her bed.

As she stared at it, the unmistakable click of a gun sounded from somewhere behind her.

She whirled around and reached for her weapon, but stopped as she saw him. He stood in the shadows by the closet, a tall, dark-haired man with broad shoulders and a gun leveled at her chest.

It was a known fact that often a murderer will revisit the scene of his crime and this man with hair as dark as midnight and hard, cold eyes the color of the gun he held in his hand, looked like he could put a bullet through her heart, then go enjoy a nice cold beer with his buddies.

"Who the hell are you?" she demanded, as if she were in a position to demand anything.

"I think that's my line." His voice was sexy deep and although his tone was relatively light, the sharp gaze of his eyes belied the easy tone.

"Special Agent Taylor, FBI," she replied.

"Sheriff Matt Buchannan, and nobody called the FBI, so what in the hell are you doing here on my crime scene?"

"I'd feel a lot better about discussing all this if you didn't have that gun pointed at me." She didn't know if he was the sheriff or the killer, but she definitely wished he'd point his gun in another direction.

"And I'd feel a lot better if you'd show me some identification and answer my questions," he replied, not lowering the gun.

Carefully Jenna reached into the back pocket of

her jeans and pulled out her identification wallet with two fingers. She had no idea how trigger happy the man might be, but she didn't want to give him any reason to fire the weapon he had in his hand.

"I'll show you mine if you show me yours," she said. He didn't look like a sheriff. His hair was too long and there was no way the T-shirt that stretched across his broad shoulders and the worn jeans that hugged the length of his long legs could be construed as an official law enforcement uniform.

He pulled a badge holder from his pocket and tossed it to the floor at her feet. She reached down and picked it up and looked at it. It was official, the man in front of her was the sheriff of Bridgewater, Texas.

When he'd eyed her identification, he finally holstered the gun and tossed the thin wallet back to her. She caught it midair with one hand and tucked it back into her pocket.

"You want to tell me what you're doing here?" He walked over to the wall and flipped on the light switch.

In the stark overhead light he was even more intimidating than he'd been with a gun in his hand. Although his features were sharp and handsome, a scar raced down one side of his face. That, along with the hard gleam in his eyes, let her know he was a man who was intimately acquaintanted with violence.

"Miranda Harris was my best friend and I'm here to catch her killer," she said and handed him back his badge.

"Unofficially, of course, because the FBI has no jurisdiction in this case. And you've already gotten on my bad side by showing up here without contacting me. I could arrest you right now for trespassing on my crime scene."

"I'm good at what I do," Jenna said. "I can help you with this."

"And what exactly is it that you do?" he asked.

"I'm a profiler."

Those hard cold eyes of his lit with a hint of amusement. "Ah, so you're going to read some books and compare evidence and magically pull a killer out of your hat?"

She stared at him for a long moment. "Are you being an ass on purpose or does it just come naturally to you?" she asked, not trying to hide her irritation. How dare he question her process, her very competence? He was nothing but a small-time sheriff with a closed, small mind.

"Folks around here say it comes pretty natural to me," he replied easily. "Now, I don't know where you came from, but I suggest you go back there before I change my mind and throw some handcuffs on you." He gestured her toward the door.

It was impossible for Jenna to argue with him. She knew she had no business being in the house. She was, indeed, trespassing on a crime scene.

She was acutely conscious of him just behind her

as she walked back down the hallway to the front door. She could smell him, the scent of clean male and a faint spicy cologne that was intensely appealing.

She knew the only way she was going to be able to gain access to the information she needed to find the person responsible for Miranda's murder was to play nice with the locals. This man was at the top of that list.

When she reached the door she turned to face him. "Look, we seem to have gotten off on the wrong foot here." She forced a smile to her lips. "I apologize for not going the official route and introducing myself before coming here, but I'm sure I could be of some help to you."

"Where are you staying?"

"The Sleepy Owl Motel," she replied, hopeful that he was going to tell her that they could work together on this.

"I'm sure I'll have some questions for you. Miranda was relatively new in town. You might know something about her that nobody else here knows." He opened the front door. "Other than answering some questions, the best thing you can do is stay out of my investigation," he said. What little amusement that had lit his slate-gray eyes was gone.

"I'd like to say it was a pleasure, Sheriff Buchannan, but it wasn't." Jenna turned and walked down the sidewalk to where she'd parked her car.

The July sunshine was hot on her shoulders, but not as warm as the heat of Sheriff Matt Buchannan's gaze on her.

She'd screwed up. She should have gone to the sheriff's office and introduced herself one professional to another before coming here to the house.

She wanted access to the files, to the interviews, to everything pertaining to Miranda's murder. Somehow she was going to have to find a way to work around Buchannan because she wasn't going anywhere until she found the man who had taken the life of her best friend.

MATT WATCHED THE FBI agent as she walked down the sidewalk to her car. He had a feeling she was a tough little piece of work, but he couldn't help but notice the sway of her shapely hips beneath the tight jeans.

He watched until she got into the driver's seat and pulled away from the curb. There was no question that she was exceptionally pretty with her long wavy chestnut hair and blue eyes that had snapped with intelligence.

She had a mouth on her, too, lush and moist and fresh as a petulant teenager. Hell, he couldn't remember the last time he'd been accused of being an ass, at least not to his face.

He had a feeling he hadn't seen the last of her. He also had a feeling that this wouldn't be the last time she'd irritate him.

She had some nerve, waltzing in here without notice or permission. She probably figured since she was a big FBI profiler that all she had to do was take a peek at the crime scene and she'd be able to solve the case.

Matt knew the case was only going to be solved by good old-fashioned investigation. This was his town. He knew the players and he didn't need some hotshot FBI agent with a personal stake in the case to muck things up.

He left the house and headed back to his office. It was a four-block walk from the crime scene. Officially he was off-duty for the day, but until the murder of Miranda Harris was solved, there was no such thing as a day off.

Bridgewater, Texas, was a small town with the traditional Main Street holding two blocks of businesses. It was a place where everyone knew everyone else, where secrets were difficult to keep. The last murder had taken place ten years ago, long before Matt had become sheriff.

Matt had seen murder before. He'd worked as a homicide cop in Chicago for seven years before returning here to his roots and he'd seen the worst that people could do to each other.

But this one bothered him in a way none of the others ever had. Miranda Harris had been an attractive twenty-nine-year-old who had moved to Bridgewater three months earlier. She'd gotten a job working at the Bridgewater Café and had been well liked by all her coworkers.

Everyone had been shocked by the news of her murder and most people believed the killer was somebody from her past. It was much easier to believe that a killer had come to Bridgewater rather than to believe that a killer belonged to Bridgewater.

Matt was a familiar sight walking the streets of his town. His home was three blocks from his office and he'd always found he did his best thinking while walking.

A hundred thoughts whirled in his head now. He definitely had some questions for Ms. FBI Profiler about Miranda. They had yet to determine next of kin, had only managed to learn that she had come from Dallas following a divorce, and so far Matt and his deputies hadn't been able to locate her ex-husband.

Maybe Jenna Taylor could fill in some blanks, could give him an idea of who from Miranda's past might want her dead.

He'd stopped by the house to spend some time alone in the room where life had been stolen, hoping that something would jump out at him, that he might see something in a new light, but the only thing new had been the arrival of Jenna Taylor.

"Hey, Harley," Matt said as he greeted the old man clipping a row of scrubs in front of his house.

"Sheriff." Harley nodded and dropped his clippers to his side. "Hot enough for you?"

"Only going to get hotter," Matt replied.

"You find that killer yet?"

"Working on it."

Harley frowned. "Forty-three years Mary and I have lived in this house and never has she asked me twice to make sure the doors are locked. But the last two nights she's had me check the locks half a dozen times. She's scared, Sheriff. Scared that some madman is going to get her like he got that young woman."

"You tell Mary we're going to get this guy. It's just a matter of time," Matt replied.

"Forty-eight hours have already passed. Doesn't that mean your best chance of getting him is gone?"

Matt stifled a groan. God help the people who watched crime shows on television and believed everything they saw. "Harley, very few crimes are solved in forty-eight hours. Trust me, we're going to solve this case." With a wave of his hand, Matt continued down the sidewalk, his thoughts even more troubled than they had been moments before.

The murder had shaken people and there were details that hadn't been released, details that made Matt's guts clench. He hoped his gut was wrong, that this was a specific, isolated murder. But he had a bad feeling.

The sheriff's office was located in the center of Main Street. It was a two-story brick building. The jail was located on the second floor and the first floor was divided into three rooms. The largest room held four desks where the deputies and the dispatcher worked. The second room was an interrogation/conference room and the third was Matt's office.

"Hey, Sheriff," Deputy Joey Kincaid greeted him as he walked through the door. The young man was the only person in the place. "Anything new?"

"Afraid not," Matt replied. Joey was the most eager-to-learn-the-ropes deputy he'd ever worked with. He was like a sponge that soaked up any knowledge Matt might have to give him about the job. And he was an unusually quiet young man who rarely spoke unless he was asking questions.

"Anything new here?" Matt asked.

Joey shook his head. "Nothing. Linda and Jim went to lunch and I've just been holding down the fort."

"I'm going to take a quick shower. If anyone calls, just take a message," Matt said and then stepped into his inner office.

The first thing he looked at was the small, framed photograph that sat on his desk. In the photo was a beautiful blonde woman, his wife.

For three years she'd been his world and then that world had been stolen away by a madman. He reached up and touched the scar on his face. It never itched unless he looked at the photograph and remembered all that he'd lost.

It had been five years since Natalie had been taken,

but there were days the wound felt as fresh as if it had just happened. Other days it felt like a dream he'd once had in another lifetime.

Matt headed to the bathroom with a shower just off his office where his uniform hung waiting. He stripped naked and stepped beneath a spray of hot water.

He worked to wash the stink of death off him before he donned his official khaki slacks and shirt. It was just after noon. He'd spend an hour or so reviewing the file on Miranda, then head out to the Sleepy Owl Motel and question Jenna Taylor.

Maybe if he conducted an official interview with her she'd be satisfied that he was doing his job and would go away.

He stepped out of the shower and dried off, then pulled on his clothes. Back at his desk he opened the pitifully thin file that contained the crime scene photos, reports of the evidence gathered and the interviews that had been conducted so far in the Miranda Harris murder case.

He didn't know how long he'd been reading when he heard the sound of voices coming from the other room. Assuming that Linda Jerrod, the dispatcher and Deputy Jim Enderly had returned from lunch, he got up to check in with them.

The minute he opened his door he saw her. Jenna Taylor, her pert butt parked almost on top of Joey's desk. The flirtatious smile that had lifted her lips slid away as Matt stepped into the room. Joey's face turned bright red and he jumped up from his desk.

"Hmm, Sheriff, this is FBI Agent Taylor. She was just asking me some questions about the Harris case," he exclaimed.

"Yes, we met earlier," Matt said and tried to hang on to the anger the sight of her had evoked. Between her badge and her beauty, she'd probably been able to twist poor Joey into a million knots.

"Joey, go to lunch," he said. "And you—" he pointed a menacing finger at Jenna "—in my office."

Chapter Two

Sheriff Matt Buchannan was livid.

Jenna could tell by the color that filled his face, making the scar on his cheek stand out in stark relief. She sat in the chair opposite his desk and waited for the explosion she knew was imminent.

He reared back in his chair and drew a deep breath. "Do you not believe in taking orders?" he asked, his voice deep and deceptively calm.

"Depends on who's giving them," she replied.

His eyes narrowed as he held her gaze. "Stay away from my deputies, and trust me, that's an order you don't want to ignore."

"I was just trying to get information about the murder. If you don't want me bothering your deputies, then let me see your file. Give me copies of the crime scene photos and any interviews that you've conducted in response to the crime. Play nice with me and I won't have a reason to go anywhere else to try to get information."

He leaned forward and pulled out a piece of paper. "How do you know Miranda?"

Jenna realized that apparently he intended to interview her and had ignored her request for the official reports of the crime. "Miranda and I have been best friends since we were twelve years old."

"Had you been in contact with her recently?"

"I spoke to her by phone the Saturday night before her death." A rise of grief welled up inside her, but she mentally shoved it away. She refused to allow herself to show any emotion in front of this man with his hard gray eyes.

"Did she mention anyone she was having problems with here in town?"

Jenna shook her head. "No, even though she'd only been here a couple of months, she loved living here. She loved working as a waitress at the café and told me she was making lots of new friends."

"What brought her here to Bridgewater?"

The heightened color had left his features and once again Jenna was struck by the fact that the sheriff was a hottie. She noticed the photo on top of his desk, a pretty blonde she assumed was his wife. She wondered what kind of a husband he was with his commanding presence and autocratic air. Probably a real pain in the butt, a his-way-or-the-highway type.

"Agent Taylor?"

She realized she hadn't answered his question. "She

was coming off a bad divorce and was looking to start over someplace new. She'd driven through here last fall and had thought it was a charming little town, and decided this was as good a place as any to start a new life."

"You said a bad divorce? Bad how?"

"Nothing violent or anything like that. Mark just didn't love her anymore, and it broke her heart when he asked for a divorce." Miranda had been devastated by the death of her marriage, but she'd also been an optimist at heart, certain that true love and happiness was just around the next corner. "I can't imagine her ex-husband having anything to do with this," she added.

"Do you know where he is? How I can contact him?"

Jenna frowned thoughtfully. "Last I heard he had moved back in with his parents. I don't know the address, but their names are John and Belinda Harris and they live on the south side of Dallas."

"What about any other next of kin? Do you know how I can contact Miranda's parents? Any siblings?" he asked.

"There is no next of kin," she replied. "Her parents are dead and she had no siblings." Except me, Jenna thought.

"Do you know her last known address?"

She told him and watched as he wrote down the information. The sunlight drifting in through the windows played in the thick darkness of his hair and she had the irrational impulse to lean forward and stroke that darkness with her fingers.

A new irritation swept through her. "Are you going to let me have those files or not?" she asked.

"Not," he replied. "You have no place in this investigation." Those cool gray eyes of his slid down the length of her. "Don't you have a job to get back to, or were you fired for insubordination?"

"I'm on a personal leave of absence, so I'm free to hang out here in Bridgewater," she replied and could tell that he wasn't pleased at the prospect.

Tough. She wasn't walking away from this. With or without his help she intended to investigate this murder. She owed it to Miranda who had been the only light in her world of darkness.

She stood, deciding she'd had enough. She had work to do and if he wasn't going to share what he knew, then she'd just have to work twice as hard to find out who was responsible for Miranda's murder.

"If you need to ask me any more questions you know where to find me," she said.

She was halfway to the door when he stopped her by calling her name. She turned back to look at him. "We found a will in Miranda's personal effects. From what I saw of it you appear to be her sole beneficiary. You might want to contact David Waller. He's the lawyer here in town and is taking care of the legalities."

Once again a wealth of emotion buoyed up inside

her. Sole beneficiary. Somehow those words made Miranda's death final as it hadn't been before.

Miranda was gone forever. Grief clawed up the back of Jenna's throat, the bitter taste nearly choking her. Never again would she see the brightness of Miranda's smile, hear her girlish giggles as she shared something funny.

Jenna turned on her heel and left. As she hurried out of the sheriff's office and into her rental car she was half-blinded by tears. She leaned her forehead against the steering wheel and gulped air in an effort to stanch her sobs.

Within moments she had successfully gained control. Control was one of the things that Jenna did best. She'd learned it early in her childhood. Don't cry. Don't show fear. Don't show any emotion at all. If you did it could be used against you if Mommy was having a bad day. And Mommy had lots of bad days.

She pulled away from the office and drove slowly down the street, checking out the businesses on either side of the road. It was mostly the usual stuff that made up small towns: post office, grocery store and city hall. There were also little specialty shops, a dress boutique, a store that sold stained-glass creations and a taxidermy shop with a stuffed wolf and a raccoon in the window that she thought was more than a little bit creepy.

The place that most interested her was the café. She pulled into an empty parking space down the street from the Bridgewater Café. Miranda had worked there before her death and Jenna hadn't had lunch.

The place would probably be packed with the lunch crowd and hopefully some of them would be chatty about Miranda and her murder.

Jenna was just about to get out of her car when her cell phone rang. She pulled it from her purse and checked the caller ID. Sam Connelly, fellow FBI profiler and friend.

"Well, if it isn't the prince of darkness," she said.

"Calling the princess," he replied. "I just wanted to check in with you and see if you were doing okay."

Warmth swept through her as she heard the concern in his deep voice. She and Sam had worked more horrible cases together than she wanted to remember. Sam was sinfully handsome and sexy, but there were absolutely no romantic sparks between them. He came from a place of darkness like she did and although that made them good friends, it also kept them from being anything more to each other. They were just too much alike.

"I'm fine," she replied. "I've made contact with the local sheriff."

"How did that go?"

"He's an ass and not only doesn't he want my help, but I also think he would gladly pay for a plane ticket to get me out of his town."

"Ah, one of those. So, what are you going to do? Are you heading back here to Kansas City?"

"No way. I just found out I'm Miranda's beneficiary, so I'll need to hang around here and take care of her estate."

"And if you happen to catch a killer while you're there, then it's all good," Sam said.

She smiled into the phone. He knew her so well. "That's the plan."

"You'll call if you need anything or if you just want to talk?" he asked.

"Of course," she replied even though they both knew she would do no such thing. "Just do me one favor," she said. "If somehow this jerk of a sheriff gets me behind bars, make sure you come and bail me out?"

Sam laughed. "You know the smart thing to do would be not anything that will make him want to lock you up."

"Yeah, but when did I ever do the smart thing?" she said and with a murmured goodbye she clicked off. She dropped the phone back into her purse and stared at the door to the café.

There was no way she believed that Miranda's killer was somebody from her past. Jenna was the kind of woman who made enemies, not Miranda. Jenna worked a job that created enemies and if that wasn't enough, her mouthiness and bad-ass attitude didn't help. There was nobody from Miranda's life before Bridgewater that Jenna could think of who would be a viable suspect.

No, the killer was here, in this picturesque little town with its quaint shops and smiling people, people who hopefully liked to gossip. And a murder would definitely be fodder for all the gossipmongers in town.

Matt Buchannan might want her out of his hair, out of his town, but Jenna didn't intend to leave here until she'd exposed the killer.

THE MOMENT MATT entered the café he saw her. Seated at the counter and chatting up Sally Cooper, one of the waitresses. Why was he not surprised?

He approached the counter and smiled at Sally. "Hey, Sally, what's the special today?" Although he didn't look at Jenna he sensed her stiffening at the sound of his voice.

"If it's Tuesday it must be meat loaf," she replied. "And we have your favorite dessert today, Sheriff. Michael whipped up a couple of lemon meringue pies this morning."

He slid onto the stool next to Jenna. "Great, then I'll have the daily special and a piece of that pie."

It was only when Sally left the counter to put in the order that Matt turned to look at the woman seated next to him. "Learn anything?"

She gestured toward the plate in front of her. "I'm scarcely halfway through my French fries, I haven't been here long enough to learn anything yet." She dragged a fry through a pool of ketchup, then popped it in her mouth. "Although I did manage to introduce myself to Sally."

Sally returned with the coffeepot and poured Matt a cup. "Anything new in the murder case?" she asked, her voice low as she leaned toward Matt.

He could almost feel Jenna holding her breath to hear his reply. "Nothing that I can talk about," he said.

Sally shook her head. "It's a scary thing. I've lived in this town fifty years and counting and I don't remember a murder like Miranda's ever taking place here. She was such a nice young woman, always smiling." Sally shook her head again and walked away to fill another customer's coffee cup.

Matt took a sip of his coffee. He'd believed Jenna was as cold as they came when they had spoken about the murder. She hadn't blinked an eye at the crime scene nor had she shown any emotion at all when sitting in his office.

Until he'd told her she was Miranda's beneficiary. It was only then that he'd seen a deepening of the blue of her eyes, a slight tremor in her full lower lip, and he'd realized she wasn't as cold and unaffected as she'd pretended to be earlier.

Sitting this close to her he could smell her, the pleasant scent of clean with a touch of something slightly citrusy.

"Doesn't your wife fix you a nice hot lunch?" she asked, breaking the silence that had welled up between them.

"My wife?"

"Yeah, I figured the picture on your desk of the pretty blonde was your wife." She half-turned to look at him.

"She was. She died five years ago."

"Sorry," she replied.

"Yeah, so am I," Matt replied. He fought the impulse to scratch his scar, the scar he'd received while wrestling with a madman, the same man who had killed Natalie.

"A man like you, surely you have a girlfriend who would be eager to fix you lunch, then."

"Agent Taylor, if I didn't know better I'd think that was a backhanded compliment," he said with a half grin.

"Good thing you know better," she replied. "And you might as well call me Jenna because I don't intend on going anywhere anytime soon." She picked up another fry. "You have to tell me something," she said as she stared down at her plate.

She looked back at him and in the depths of her eyes he saw a shimmer of pain. "I wasn't given any real information before coming here, just that she'd been murdered. I need to know the details. They can't be any worse than my imagination." She broke off as Sally arrived with his plate of food.

"I don't want to talk about it here," he said. He supposed there were some things he could tell her that wouldn't compromise his investigation, although there were some details that hadn't been shared with anyone and he wasn't about to share those with her.

"Then where?" she replied.

"Why don't we finish our lunch and then I'll follow you back to your motel room. We can talk there without interruption, without anyone listening."

"Thank you," she said and focused back on her plate.

"Where are you from?" he asked.

"A little town just north of Kansas City. I work out of the Kansas City field office."

"Married?"

"Nope."

"Do you have a significant other?" he asked.

"Yeah, a cranky cat that showed up half-dead on my doorstep." She gazed at him with narrowed eyes. "What's this? Be nice to the FBI agent and maybe she'll go away?"

"Something like that," Matt agreed easily.

"It doesn't matter whether you're nice or mean to me, I'm here for the long haul," she replied.

"Won't your cat miss you?"

"Nah, we have no emotional attachment to each other. That's why we get along so well. I have a friend who is taking care of her while I'm gone."

The statement was definitely telling. He suspected

that this was a woman who didn't play well with others. What she had to realize was that when it came to an ongoing murder investigation in his town, he wasn't willing to play well with her.

Plus, he wasn't at all sure he believed in the whole profiling thing. As far as he was concerned, solving a crime happened only one way—through intensive investigation, intelligent interrogation and exhaustive interviews.

He thought profiling was a bit of hocus-pocus that might work in the case of serial killers, but there was absolutely nothing in the Harris murder that indicated this was anything but an isolated crime.

"How long have you been Sheriff here?"

"Almost five years. Before that I was a homicide cop in Chicago."

She looked at him in surprise. "Really, what brought you to this tiny town?"

"I was born and raised here, but moved to Chicago to join the police force. I came back here after the death of my wife. It so happened that the sheriff was retiring, so I stepped into his shoes."

There had been a time when he couldn't talk about his wife, when even thinking about her brought a pain that nearly cast him to his knees. But that terrible grief had passed and over the last year he'd finally begun to look forward instead of backward.

For the next few minutes they ate in silence. She finished her meal but made no move to leave.

There was a part of him, a strictly male part, that found Special Agent Jenna Taylor extremely attractive. Definitely a fatal attraction, he told himself ruefully.

"Why didn't you tell me about being Miranda's beneficiary when you first met me?" she asked.

He eyed her with a touch of amusement. "If you'll recall we didn't exactly meet under the best of circumstances. I was trying to decide if I should arrest you for interfering with a crime scene."

"I didn't touch anything. I'm not exactly a novice around crime scenes." She leaned closer to him and he couldn't help but notice that she had the most kissable-looking lips he'd seen in a long time. "I could help you, you know. Catching killers is what I do for a living, it's who I am."

He finished the last bite of his meat loaf and then pushed his plate away. "If you really want to help me, then tell me a little bit about Miranda. You said the two of you were best friends. I didn't know her personally, so any information you can tell me about the kind of person she was would help. You said you've known her since she was twelve, did the two of you meet in school?"

"No, Miranda's parents brought me into their home as a foster child, but that was a long time ago," she said with a touch of impatience. "Miranda and I were like sisters."

"You look a lot like her," he said.

For the first time since he'd met her she smiled, a

real smile that warmed the blue of her eyes and lit her features from within. An unexpected flicker of desire ignited in the pit of his stomach.

"Miranda and I used to tell people that we were fraternal twins, not exactly alike but almost. We might have looked alike but in most things we were polar opposites."

"How so?" he asked curiously.

"Miranda was like a big ball of sunshine. She never met anyone she didn't like, believed that everyone had some good inside them."

"And you don't believe that?"

"It's my job to look for the darkness in everyone," she replied ruefully.

They fell silent as Sally brought Matt his lemon pie. Jenna slid off her stool and placed money on the counter. "Look, I'm going to head back to my motel room. I'm in unit seven. I'll see you there in a few minutes?"

Matt nodded, then turned and watched her weave her way through the tables to the front door. He had to admit she intrigued him more than a little bit.

Certainly that rivulet of desire that he'd momentarily felt had stunned him. He hadn't felt that for any woman for over five years. Just his luck that the first woman who stirred him on a physical level was one he didn't think he even liked much.

Chapter Three

Jenna paced the short length of floor in front of the window of the small motel room window. It had been thirty minutes since she'd left the café. How long could it take him to eat a piece of pie?

Although she knew it would be painful, she needed to hear the details of Miranda's death. She wanted to know how she'd died, who had found her body and what had been done since then to find the guilty.

She walked over to the small table where she had a notebook opened, ready to take notes. She had a laptop, but preferred handwriting things first, then transferring them to the computer. She felt like she thought better in longhand.

She flipped the pages to her to-do list and wrote down that she needed to visit the lawyer first thing in the morning. As Miranda's beneficiary she'd have to figure out what to do with the house and all of Miranda's personal belongings. The sooner she got started the better. She didn't intend to stick around this place forever.

Sinking down in a chair at the table, she pressed her fingers into the center of her forehead where a head-ache threatened to blossom.

Stress. She'd suffered from stress headaches since she'd been little. Certainly the first twelve years of her life had been filled with stresses that children should never have to experience.

Sometimes she thought those early years of her life had formed the kind of woman she'd become, a woman who sought the darkness in others because she'd come from such a dark place.

She jumped up from the chair as she heard a car door slam outside. A glance out the window showed her Matt walking toward her unit. He walked with a slightly self-confident swagger that was both attractive and more than a little bit sexy.

She opened the door before he could knock. "How was your pie?"

"Excellent," he replied as he stepped through the door.

She gestured him toward the table and suddenly felt a bit awkward. She'd been in a hundred motel rooms over the last year, but she couldn't remember the last time she'd had a hunky male in the room with her.

She sank down in front of her notebook and picked up her pen. "I hope you don't mind if I take some notes."

He shrugged his broad shoulders as he sat in the chair opposite hers. "Suit yourself." His gray eyes studied her as if she were a particularly intriguing specimen. "I'm not sure why you want to put yourself through all the gory details."

"My world is made up of gory details," she replied.

"I hope you have something good to balance that."

Miranda, she thought. Miranda had been her balance and now she was gone. "Let's just get down to business," she said briskly. "She was stabbed, wasn't she?"

He looked at her in surprise. "How did you know that?"

"I saw the mattress on the bed, the bloodstains. No bullet holes, just blood. There was no castoff on the walls, so she wasn't bludgeoned."

He nodded. "She was stabbed. Several times through the heart. There was no sign of forced entry, so we can only assume she might have known the killer." He kept his voice low and steady as he dryly recited the facts. "She was killed sometime in the early hours of Sunday morning. When she didn't show up for the lunch shift, Michael Brown, the owner of the café, got concerned and sent over one of the waitresses to check on her."

"What's the waitress's name?" she asked.

"Maggie Wendt. Apparently she and Miranda had become quite close friends. Miranda had given Maggie a key to her house. When Maggie got there and saw Miranda's car in the driveway but she didn't answer the door, Maggie got worried and went inside."

"You checked out her story?"

"Thoroughly. The whole thing has practically destroyed her. I don't think she's left her house since she found Miranda."

"Any other suspects?" she asked.

"I was hoping you'd be able to give me some names. She was only in town for three months. I can't help but think it's possible that somebody from her past is responsible for this."

Jenna frowned thoughtfully. "I can't imagine it."

"But you said you live in Kansas City and Miranda was living in Dallas before moving here. Maybe there were things about her life that she didn't share with you?"

Was it possible? Were there secrets in Miranda's life, secrets she hadn't shared with Jenna? "You just don't want to believe that the killer might be home-grown," she said.

He smiled and nodded. Oh, the man had a nice, sexy smile. "Of course I don't want to believe that anyone from Bridgewater is capable of such a crime, but my mind is certainly open to the possibility."

"When is the house going to be released?"

He frowned, but the gesture did nothing to diminish his handsomeness. "Probably sometime tomorrow afternoon. We've already collected all the evidence, what little there was, but I was going to do another walk through in the morning."

"What kind of evidence did you collect?" she asked.

Once again he frowned. "Unfortunately not much. There wasn't a single fingerprint anywhere in the house except for Miranda's."

"So the killer wiped everything down," she said. "Or he wore gloves."

"We didn't get much of anything that would help the investigation." His gaze shifted from hers for a moment, making her believe he wasn't telling her the whole truth. "Why do you want to know when the house will be released?"

"I need to take care of packing things, but also as soon as you release it I'll be staying there."

He raised a dark eyebrow. "Won't that be difficult for you?"

"Why? Because she died there?" Jenna set down her ink pen. "She also lived there." To Jenna's horror a mist of unexpected tears filled her eyes. She stared down at the table and drew several deep breaths in an effort to regain control of her emotions.

He reached out a hand and covered one of hers. "I'm sorry, Jenna. I'm sorry about your friend."

Three things sprang to her mind. The first was a black grief for the friend she had lost. The second was that she liked the way her name sounded falling from his lips. The third was that the touch of his big, strong hand shot a wave of evocative warmth up her arm.

She pulled her hand from his and looked at him. "It's been five years since you've investigated a murder, something like this. Aren't you worried that you might be a little rusty?"

He smiled again, that sexy, easy half grin. "It's kind of like making love. Even if it's been a long time you never forget how to do it."

Her mind exploded with a vision of him in bed, naked and with hunger shining from his gray eyes. She consciously willed the vision away and narrowed her eyes. His statement had been totally inappropriate and she had a feeling he'd done it on purpose, in an effort to throw her off balance and replace her grief with irritation. She had a feeling Sheriff Matt Buchannan was far more intelligent than she'd given him credit for.

She suddenly wanted him out of her motel room, as far away from her as possible. It was clear he didn't intend to share any real information with her, clear that he wasn't going to help her in her investigation of Miranda's murder. And there was something about his easy smile, his very attractiveness that was somehow threatening to her.

"I'll give you my cell phone number and I'd appreciate it if you would call me when I can get into the house," she said.

She wrote down her number and tore it from the notebook, then handed it to him and stood in an obvious attempt to dismiss him. "I guess we're done here."

He rose to his feet, obviously getting the clue that she was finished with him. She walked with him to the motel room door and stepped outside into the warm July air.

"Jenna, this town and this murder investigation isn't big enough for us to share. Take care of whatever you need to with Miranda's estate, but leave the investigation to me." With these words he left her and walked to his car without a backward glance.

She watched as he got into his patrol car and left the parking lot. She leaned against the outside of her unit and closed her eyes against the bright sunshine.

Miranda, what happened here? Again a wealth of grief clawed up the back of her throat, but she swallowed hard against it.

Who did you meet that killed you? Who could have plunged a knife through your loving, kind heart? Who could have hated you that much? And why? Why did this happen to you?

A faint chill swept through her despite the warmth of the sun. She had felt the creepy feeling she was being watched.

She opened her eyes and gazed around as the disturbing sensation continued. She saw nobody around, but couldn't dispel the feeling that somebody was nearby, staring at her with malevolence.

The killer?

She'd only introduced herself to Sally. Had the waitress talked about the FBI agent who had come to town? Did the killer already know she was here? Was he stalking her like she intended to stalk him?

"Bring it on," she whispered just beneath her breath as she went back into her room and locked the door behind her.

"JOEY, I'M HEADING OVER to Maggie Wendt's place for another interview," Matt said to his young deputy the next morning. "If you need me, you can either reach me by radio or by my cell phone."

"Got it," Joey said.

Matt left the office and stepped out into the hot morning air. Not even nine o'clock yet and the sun was already a fireball in the sky.

That wasn't all that was hot this morning. As he thought of the dream he'd had the night before, his temperature raised several notches.

Special Agent Jenna Taylor had been the center of his dream, beckoning him into bed with her mysterious blue eyes and a smile that had heated his blood to the boiling point. And he'd been a willing participant, tumbling into the sheets with her and making hot, wild love.

He got into his patrol car and started the engine. It had been a long time since he'd thought about sex, let alone had a dream where he'd awakened panting and aroused and wanting to remain asleep to experience it all over again.

It was an indication that the grief he'd suffered for so long had truly passed. He would forever hold Natalie in his heart, but she was gone and he was ready to move on.

He was only thirty-five years old, far too young to contemplate living the rest of his life alone. Besides, he knew what it was to love. He knew what it felt like to be in love and he wanted that again.

Why he'd dreamed of Jenna was a mystery to him. She'd been in town only twenty-four hours and already he found her to be a major pain.

He shoved away thoughts of Jenna and instead focused on the matter at hand. He'd done an initial interview with Maggie immediately after she'd found Miranda's body, but she'd been so distraught that he'd had to call a halt to the interview.

He'd tried to talk to her the day before as well, but she'd indicated that she was still too upset to talk about her murdered friend.

He was hoping that today she'd be able to discuss what she knew about Miranda, might be able to give him some details about the murdered woman's life that would help him find her killer.

It concerned him that they had so little to go on. None of Miranda's neighbors had seen or heard anything on the morning of her death. The only real evidence they had was a vase of roses, five long-stem roses in various stages of bloom and the sixth that had been found on the center of her bloody chest.

Nobody knew about the roses except the officers who had processed the scene. He and his team were trying to chase down where the roses might have come from, but with Bridgewater being only forty miles from Dallas, it was possible they were bought in the bigger city where there were hundreds of florists. It could take weeks or even months to chase down that particular lead.

He hadn't wanted to admit to Jenna just how little they had, just how stymied he was in finding the killer. The last five years it had been easy to be sheriff in Bridgewater. The worst of the crimes were an occasional robbery, bar fights and domestic disputes. Murder hadn't been an issue until now.

Maggie Wendt lived in a small rental home three blocks from Miranda's house. When Matt pulled up in front of it he muttered a curse as he saw the familiar rental car in the driveway. The woman who had visited his dream the night before seemed definitely determined to get on his bad side.

Even though he was irritated that she was here, he couldn't help but feel a grudging admiration for her sheer tenacity. Wouldn't he be doing the same thing if his best friend had been murdered?

He knocked on the door and Maggie answered. "Sheriff Buchannan," she said in surprise. "Please, come in. I was just speaking with your partner."

His partner? He shook his head ruefully as he followed Maggie through the small living room and into the kitchen where Jenna sat at the table with a cup of coffee in front of her.

Her eyes widened slightly at the sight of him but she offered him, a bright smile as if they were best buddies. "Sheriff, I was just chatting with Maggie," she said.

She was dressed in a pair of jeans and a sleeveless blue blouse that exactly matched her eyes. The top two buttons of the blouse were unfastened, giving him a glimpse of creamy breasts as she leaned forward to wrap her fingers around her coffee mug.

"I'm so glad you've called in the FBI," Maggie exclaimed. "I want everyone in the world looking for Miranda's killer." She gestured Matt into a chair at the table next to Jenna. "Let me get you some coffee," she said.

"Thanks, that sounds good."

As Maggie went to the coffeepot on the countertop, Matt looked at Jenna. She shrugged, as if to say that she couldn't help herself.

"I was just telling Agent Taylor what a wonderful friend Miranda was for the three months that I knew her," Maggie said as she set a cup of coffee in front of

Matt. "Everyone at the café loved her and she and I clicked right away."

Maggie joined them at the table and grabbed a napkin from the bright red rooster-shaped napkin holder in the center of the table. "I can't get the picture of her out of my head, her lying on the bed covered in blood."

Jenna reached across the table and patted Maggie's hand. "Eventually you'll forget the horror of it. Time will help."

Maggie nodded. "It's just still so fresh."

"Maggie, I know I asked you this before, but you've had a couple of days to think about things, can you think of anyone who might have been angry with Miranda? Somebody here in town who was giving her problems?"

Maggie shook her head as tears glimmered in her eyes. She unfolded the napkin and used it to dab at her tears. "I know everyone at the café loved her. She never complained, even when she took extra shifts. The customers all loved her. I can't imagine anyone wanting to hurt her. Maybe it was a robbery?" she asked hopefully, as if somehow that would make it all better.

Matt shook his head. "As far as we could tell nothing was stolen."

"Did she mention anyone she was interested in? Maybe a man who'd caught her eye?" Jenna asked.

"No, although she did tell me she thought somebody was interested in her, kind of like a secret admirer."

Jenna sat up straighter in her chair. "A secret admirer? Why would she think that?"

Maggie shrugged, but Matt had a feeling he knew the answer. The roses. Somehow the roses were the key, but damned if he could figure it out.

"She didn't go into any details, but we spent some time speculating on who might have a crush on her," Maggie said.

"And who did you come up with?" Jenna asked as she pulled a small pad and pen from her purse.

"Oh, it was just pure speculation," Maggie said. "We thought it might be Leroy Banks." She looked at Matt. "You know he works as a busboy and cook at the café. Then we thought it might be Doc Johnson. When Miranda began working at the café he started coming in for both lunch and dinner and he always sat in her section."

Jenna wrote down both names, her brow furrowed in thought. "Anyone else?" she asked as she looked at Maggie once again.

Matt leaned back in his chair and took a sip of his coffee, content to let her do the talking. She'd obviously established a rapport with Maggie before he'd arrived and if she wanted to do his work for him, at least for the moment, he wasn't complaining.

"Bud Carlson. He's kind of a jerk, he has that whole

bad-boy thing going on, but Miranda told me she thought he was kind of sexy."

"Did he act like he liked her?" Jenna asked.

Maggie frowned. "Bud flirted with her a lot. I told her that he was bad news and she should stay away from him." Once again tears filled her eyes. "Do you think Bud did this to her?"

Matt sat up straighter in his chair. "Maggie, we have no evidence to suggest that Bud had anything to do with it." The last thing he wanted or needed was for rumors to start swirling around and fingers pointing at a man who might be innocent.

"I don't know what else to tell you," Maggie said, directing her gaze to Jenna. "I've done nothing but think about this since the minute I found her dead, but I can't think of anything else that might help."

Once again Jenna reached across the table and took Maggie's hand in hers. "You've been a big help, Maggie." She smiled warmly and Matt felt the power of that smile igniting a tiny fire in the pit of his stomach.

Jenna looked at Matt. "You have anything you want to ask, Sheriff?"

He found it oddly amusing that somehow she had taken control and cast him in the role of second banana. "No, I think you've pretty much taken care of things." He got up from the table and Jenna and Maggie did the same.

"Thanks for the coffee, Maggie," he said as they reached the front door.

He wasn't surprised when Maggie reached out to hug Jenna. What surprised him was the play of emotions that swept across Jenna's face as she returned the hug. Raw and vulnerable, they flashed for just a moment and then were gone as she stepped back from Maggie.

"We'll be in touch," she said and then she stepped out of the door.

Matt fell into step beside her as they went down the sidewalk. "Partner, huh?"

"I didn't tell her that, she just assumed it," she said without apology. As they reached her car she leaned against the driver's door. "Tell me about the men she mentioned. I can't believe she didn't say anything to me about a secret admirer."

"Maybe she was waiting until she knew who it was before talking to you about it," he said and then continued. "Leroy Banks is a thirty-year-old who works as a busboy. He's the nephew of Michael Brown, the owner of the café. He moved here about six months ago."

Matt tried not to notice how the sun sparked in her hair, making it look soft and touchable. Standing this close to her he could smell her scent, that pleasant clean, citrus fragrance that he'd noticed before.

"Doc Johnson is actually Patrick Johnson, our local

veterinarian," he continued. "He's thirty-four and has always been a stand-up kind of guy. His office is next door to the café. Bud Carlson is in his late twenties, owns his own home improvement business and considers himself something of a ladies' man."

He frowned as he thought of Bud. "He drinks too much, has a hot temper and is the first one to look for a fight."

"Have you talked to any of these three?" she asked.

"No, I didn't know about them having anything to do with Miranda. You got more out of Maggie over a cup of coffee than I got in an hour-long interview just after the murder." He fought against a sigh of frustration.

Before she could reply his cell phone rang. He pulled it from his pocket and answered.

"Sheriff, it's Joey. I just got a call from George Hudson. He was hysterical, said Carolyn Cox is dead—murdered. He told me she was in her bed and she'd been stabbed. It sounds like the other one, just like Miranda's murder."

Matt's stomach clenched tightly. "I'm on my way. Get Thad and Jerry to meet me there." He clicked off the phone and dropped it back into his pocket.

"What?" Jenna asked.

"It looks like we might have another murder," he said.

"I'll follow you," she replied, as if there were no question that she was coming along.

He didn't have time to argue with her, nor was he

sure he wanted to. If the information that Joey had given him was true, it meant Miranda Harris wasn't an isolated case. It was quite possible that a serial killer was working in his town.

Chapter Four

Jenna followed Matt's car, her heart thudding a familiar rhythm. It was the rhythm of the hunt. If what Matt said was true, then there was a killer in this town, somebody who had killed not once, but twice.

She caught killers. That's what she did. If this murder was anything like Miranda's, then surely Matt wouldn't turn down her offer to help now.

He pulled up in front of an attractive duplex where a man was seated in the middle of the front yard sobbing. He pulled himself to his feet as Matt got out of his car and approached. Jenna parked just behind Matt's vehicle and also got out.

"She's dead, oh God, she's dead," the man sobbed, then reeled sideways and retched onto the grass. "She'd invited me to have breakfast with her. I got here and the door was unlocked, so I went in." Each word came on a pained gasp and by that time a patrol car had arrived and two deputies got out.

"Jerry, take care of George, and Thad, get Raymond and Justin here, then start canvassing the area to see if any of the neighbors saw or heard anything." Matt barked the orders sharply, his features taut with tension.

He went to the back of his car and opened the trunk, then pulled out a pair of gloves and booties. Jenna joined him there and looked at him expectantly. He pulled a second pair of gloves and booties from the trunk and handed them to her.

He didn't say a word as she followed him to the front porch. There they put on the crime scene gear, then entered into a small, neat living room.

"Carolyn Cox," he said as he looked around. "I think she's twenty-eight or twenty-nine years old and works as a dental assistant."

As he filled her in, Jenna looked around the room, knowing that every square inch of the duplex had the potential of containing a clue.

He went directly down the hallway and peeked into the master bedroom, then looked back at her and shook his head and returned to where she stood.

"No need for an ambulance," he said and began to look around the room where they stood.

She was pleased that he seemed to work the way she did, slowly and methodically, not rushing into where the body was but rather allowing the scene to speak to him in subtle nuances.

"No sign of a struggle," he said more to himself than to her. "No sign of forced entry at the front door." He walked over to the two living room windows. "Both locked."

She followed him into the kitchen, equally as neat and tidy as the living room had been. Carolyn Cox might have intended to have a breakfast guest, but she'd never gotten a chance to start the preparations for a meal. The only thing on the table was a vase of long-stem red roses, roses that Matt stared at for a long moment as a muscle in his jaw worked overtime.

"Let's go see our victim and the scene of the crime," he finally said.

She nodded and steeled herself for death. The scent of it hung in the air as they went down the hallway. It was a smell more familiar to Jenna than the scent of her own mother.

Matt paused in front of the master bedroom. "You okay?" he asked.

"Right as rain," she replied and then they both stepped into the room.

Jenna couldn't help the small gasp that escaped her as she saw the victim. Carolyn Cox in life had been an attractive brunette with blue eyes. She was clad in a pair of summer pajamas, the center of the blouse saturated with blood. On top of the blood sat a single red rose.

Jenna shot a quick glance at Matt. "Is this how

you found Miranda?" she asked. "With the rose on her chest?"

He gave a curt nod as he stepped closer to the bed. "She doesn't appear to have any defensive wounds."

"So, was she killed while sleeping or did she get up and answer the door?"

"We'll know more after Justin gets here," he replied.

"Justin?"

"Our local undertaker and working coroner," he said. He backed away from the bed and surveyed the room. Jenna walked over to the window and noted that it was locked.

Jenna found herself looking everywhere but at the victim, afraid that Miranda's face would be superimposed over Carolyn's in her mind. "I'm going to check all the other windows in the house."

He nodded and she left the room. As she checked the other windows her mind whirled. The killer had staged the body with a rose. The rose meant something, but what?

Behavioral analysis, that's what she did best. Somehow she had to take the behavior and study it and come up with a profile that would help identify the killer. It was a high-stakes mind game with the built-in time line of catching him before he killed again.

If the same person had killed both Miranda and Carolyn, then there had been only three days between the crimes. That short period of time was both unusual and unsettling.

She returned to the bedroom where Matt stood at the foot of the bed, taking notes in a pad, his expression grim. "My boys are here to take the crime scene photos and collect evidence." He closed the pad and looked at her, his eyes a flat metal gray that gave nothing away. "You said you wanted to be involved in this. If you're still offering, then I'm accepting."

"Then I'm in," she said, pleased that he was a man who was strong enough to ask for help. "I'll need to see everything you have from Miranda's case and of course everything we get from this one."

"Done."

At that moment two deputies entered the room with their evidence collection kits. As they began their work, Jenna and Matt went outside to interview George.

It was nearing dusk when everything that could be done had been done at the scene. Carolyn's body had been taken away, the neighborhood had been canvassed for anyone who might have seen anything and interviews had been finished.

Jenna and Matt were walking toward their cars when her stomach growled so loudly she knew he'd heard it. "You missed lunch," he said.

"I missed breakfast and lunch," she replied.

"Want to grab a bite at the café? Maybe we can catch

up with Leroy there and ask him a few questions while we're at it," he suggested.

"Sounds good," she agreed. "I'll meet you there."

Minutes later as she drove toward the café she thought about what she'd learned about Matt Buchannan over the course of the afternoon.

It had been obvious that the men who worked for him not only respected him but also wanted to please him. It spoke well of his ability to lead.

She'd watched him directing his men in the evidence collection and hadn't been able to find fault. Her initial assessment of him as a small-town incompetent had completely turned around. The man was sharp and focused and had been one step ahead of her all afternoon.

The dinner rush was gone by the time she and Matt walked into the café. He gestured her toward a table in the back where they would have more privacy to talk.

A big burly man ambled out of the kitchen to their table. "Hey, Matt," he said as he wiped his hands on his white apron. "Heard you've had a rough day."

"I guess news travels fast," Matt replied. "This is FBI Special Agent Jenna Taylor. Jenna, this is the owner of this place, Michael Brown."

"Nice to meet you," Michael said. "So, you've called in the FBI?" he asked Matt.

"I'm here unofficially," Jenna replied. "I was a friend of Miranda Harris."

Michael winced. "I'm sorry for your loss. Hell, I'm sorry for my loss. She was a keeper, that one."

"Leroy working tonight?" Matt asked.

"Yeah, he's back in the kitchen washing dishes. Why?" Michael's friendly smile became more guarded.

"We'd like to have a little chat with him," Jenna said. She offered the big man a sweet smile. "We're speaking with everyone who worked here with Miranda."

"I'll have him come out and talk to you. In the meantime what can I get you to eat?" He took their orders and then headed back toward the kitchen.

"You questioned him?" Jenna asked Matt.

"Michael was one of the first people I talked to. I figured he'd know better than anyone if Miranda was having any problems with her coworkers."

"You know this has all the earmarks of a serial," she said softly.

"Officially it take three deaths to qualify as a serial," he replied.

Again he'd surprised her with his knowledge. "That's true, but in both cases there's an element of a ritual. Were there any drugs found in Miranda's system?"

"The toxicology screens haven't come back yet," he replied. "Why?"

"I'm trying to figure out how somebody would subdue those women in their beds and stab them. He either had to be big enough to overwhelm them or use a gun or some other weapon to control them." Her mind worked to make sense of what little they knew, but she just didn't have enough information yet.

"Actually, there were ligature marks around Miranda's wrists and ankles. They were on Carolyn as well."

She looked at him in dismay. "First the roses, now this. Is there anything else you've neglected to mention?"

"Just that I think you have a really pretty smile and that you should smile more often."

His words hit her out of left field and to her surprise she felt the warmth of a blush stealing over her face. Before she could form an intelligent reply, a gangly young man approached their table.

"Leroy," Matt said and kicked out an empty chair at the table. "Have a seat, we'd like to talk to you for a minute."

Leroy Banks had the bad skin of a teenager and the weary gaze of somebody much older than his years. He sank down on the chair and eyed them both warily. "Am I in trouble?"

"I don't know, have you done anything that would put you in trouble?" Matt countered.

He squirmed in his chair, as if finding their scrutiny intensely uncomfortable. "Not that I can think of, but Uncle Michael says I don't think enough."

"I'm sure that's not true," Jenna said and forced a smile. "I heard you were very nice and thoughtful to Miranda Harris."

A spasm of pain raced across his features and the

tips of his ears turned pink. "She is…was easy to be nice to. She was the nicest woman I've ever known and I can't believe somebody murdered her."

"Where were you on the morning of her murder?" Matt asked.

"Here. I'm always here. I open up in the mornings around five and I'm usually the last one here at night to close up. It's pretty much that way every day seven days a week," Leroy exclaimed.

As Matt asked him about his whereabouts that morning, she tried to concentrate on the conversation, but found herself instead focused on the man conducting it.

He thought she had a pretty smile and she thought he was hot as hell. It had been a long time since she'd felt a spark of electricity for any man, but she definitely felt it for Sheriff Matt Buchannan.

Now, all she had to do was figure out what, if anything she intended to do about it.

"THIS IS EVERYTHING I'VE got on Miranda so far," Matt said as he handed Jenna a file. It was just after seven the next morning and Jenna was seated in the small conference room in the sheriff's office.

She had her hair pulled back at her nape, exposing her graceful neck and emphasizing her cheekbones and round eyes. Clad in a pair of jeans and a turquoise T-shirt that hugged her slender curves, she looked fresh and sexy.

"I've got some administrative things to take care of in my office this morning, so I'll just leave you to it and will check back in with you in about an hour," he said.

She laid her hand on top of the file, as if reluctant to open it and looked up at him. "We're going to get this guy, aren't we, Matt?"

For the first time since he'd met her there was a touch of vulnerability in her eyes, in the slight tremor of her sexy full lower lip. "Are you sure you're okay to do this?" he asked, knowing how difficult it would be for her to view the details of her friend's murder.

She removed her hand from the top of the manila folder. "I have to be okay," she replied. "I dreamed about Miranda last night and she was begging me to find her killer." She sat up straighter in the chair, her eyes taking on a hard glint. "Both Carolyn and Miranda deserve justice and I intend to help get it for them." She waved him toward the door. "Go, I'm fine."

He left her there and went into his office where he had paperwork to take care of. Even when crime struck there were certain duties he couldn't ignore as sheriff of the town.

After dinner the night before, he and Jenna had gone in search of Bud Carlson and Doc Johnson, wanting to interview them both.

They'd found Doc Johnson at his home and had spoken with him about Miranda and Carolyn. His alibi for the time of the murders was much like Leroy's.

He'd been in bed alone when both of the women had been killed. They hadn't been able to catch up with Bud Carlson and he was on Matt's to-do list for today.

When they hadn't found Bud, they spent several hours talking to Carolyn's friends and family, but just as with Miranda nobody had any clue who might have wanted the pretty young woman dead.

George's alibi had been that, at the time of Carolyn's death, he'd been at his father's house having coffee. His father, who lived alone and suffered from insomnia often called George to come over in the wee hours of the morning.

As Matt's deputies arrived, he assigned them each duties relating to the crimes. Jenna was right about one thing, these weren't isolated incidences and they appeared to be committed by a man working out some sort of fantasy or something in his mind.

The roses. What did they mean? They were obviously an important key as to why the murders had occurred, an important clue to who might be responsible.

It was a little over an hour later when Matt got up from his desk, poured two cups of coffee, then returned to the conference room.

The moment he walked in he felt the grief hanging in the air, saw the telltale redness of her eyes that let him know she'd been weeping. His heart crunched. He knew grief intimately. He set the coffee cups on the desk as she rose from the table and quickly swiped at her eyes.

Without conscious thought he opened his arms to her and was vaguely surprised when she stepped into his embrace. She fit neatly against him, her head just beneath his chin and even though he knew it wasn't the time or the place, he couldn't help the flare of desire that rose up inside him.

He felt her heartbeat against him as she pressed her face into the front of his shirt. Her shoulders shook with a barely contained sob and he rubbed his hands up and down her back in an effort to soothe.

She stood perfectly still for a long moment, then raised her head to look up at him. It wasn't a conscious thought that drove him to lower his head and capture her lips with his. He was driven by sheer want, a crazy need.

As he tasted the warmth of her lips, he half expected her to push him away, to be outraged, but instead she wound her arms around his neck and opened her mouth to him.

She touched his tongue with hers and in that moment his effort to comfort turned into something altogether different. He stiffened slightly as he remembered they were in the conference room where anyone could walk in.

She must have felt him tense for she instantly stepped out of his arms. "Sorry, I didn't mean for that to happen," she said.

He smiled at her. "I meant it to happen sooner or later, just not here and now."

She looked at him in surprise and then offered him a rueful smile. "I don't know exactly what you're looking for Matt, but I'm pretty sure I'm not it."

He eyed her curiously. "Why would you say that?"

She went back to the table and sat. "According to my last lover I'm selfish and closed-off and completely dysfunctional in a relationship. So, I'm definitely not the right woman for anything you might have in mind."

"Or he was definitely the wrong man," Matt replied lightly. What are you doing, man, he thought. What was he doing flirting with a woman he scarcely knew, one who was only in his world because her friend had been brutally murdered?

He joined her at the table and gestured toward the file. "Did you see anything that gave you any hint of what we're up against here?" he asked.

She frowned thoughtfully. "Our killer is obviously organized and methodical. I would guess that he knew both victims."

"In a town this small that doesn't help us much," he said.

"You're checking into the roses? They appear to be floral-shop quality."

He could almost forget the kiss as he concentrated on the conversation. Almost, but not quite. "They didn't come from a floral shop here in town. I have one of my deputies checking with floral shops within a fifty-mile radius of here, but that includes Dallas. We might never know where those flowers are from."

"But they're important. We know George didn't give Carolyn those roses and there were six at both of the crime scenes, five in a vase and one left on the chest of the victim. Six roses, not a dozen. It means something to the killer, but I can't get a handle on it. If you don't mind I'll take home copies of everything you have tonight and see if I can work up some sort of profile." She looked at her watch. "I've got a meeting with that lawyer in fifteen minutes to do whatever needs to be done about Miranda's estate."

"You can get into her house anytime," he said. "We've gone over it with a fine-tooth comb."

"Thanks, then maybe after my appointment I'll check out of the motel and move my things into the house."

"Are you sure you want to do that? What if the killer returns to the scene of the crime?"

Her eyes glinted with a hardness. "Then I'll be ready for him. What are your plans?"

"I want to catch up with Bud Carlson and will continue the investigation of Carolyn's friends and family." The kiss was forgotten as they talked for several more minutes about the crimes.

"Why don't we plan on meeting up at the café for dinner and you can tell me what you learned from Bud," she suggested as she once again got up from the table.

"All right. How about we meet at around five? I'll make sure I have copies of everything for you then."

She nodded and went out the door, leaving behind only that heavenly scent that had the capacity to drive him half-mad.

He sank down at the table and raked a hand through his hair, wondering what had possessed him to kiss her? It had been over five years since he'd kissed any woman. For several years after Natalie's death the idea of being with another woman had been repugnant.

When he'd started believing that he could love again, none of the women in the small town had interested him. Over the last year he'd had several casual dates, but nobody had affected him on a visceral level like Jenna did.

Just his luck that he'd have the hots for a tough FBI agent who was only in town temporarily, a woman who'd already told him she was a mess when it came to personal relationships.

He got up and focused instead on what was important, the fact that he had two murders to solve.

Minutes later as he drove down the streets of Bridgewater his stomach clenched as he thought about the killer. There was no question now that the killer hadn't come from Miranda's past but rather was somebody here in town, somebody he knew and perhaps somebody he'd drank coffee with in the café or chatted with on the streets.

He had Joey looking into points of intersection in the two victims' lives. Had they gone to the same dentist? Used the same delivery service? It was a given that they'd probably shopped at the same grocery store and used the same beauty shop, because there were only one of each of those businesses in town. Still, there had to be something, some minute connection that could provide a clue.

Although Bud Carlson hadn't been home the night before when he and Jenna had tried to catch up with the man, Matt knew where to find him this morning. Matt had heard through the grapevine that Bud had been working on remodeling a room in the Jeffers' home.

Tom and Carrie Jeffers lived in one of the larger homes in Bridgewater, an old stone two-story with a wraparound porch and on a heavily treed large corner lot.

Bud's blue pickup was in the driveway and Matt pulled in just behind it. Carrie Jeffers answered his knock. She was a pretty blonde who worked part-time at the library.

"Sheriff, is something wrong?" she asked, her brow wrinkled with worry.

"No, I just need to speak with Bud," Matt replied.

Carrie opened her door and allowed Matt in. "He's in the back room." Her words were punctuated by the sound of a hammer banging. "Just follow the noise," she said.

Matt walked through the formal living room and into a room that was a family room. Bud Carlson stood with his back to Matt, hammering nails into a piece of Sheetrock. He was shirtless, his body lean and ripcord taut.

When he'd finished pounding the nail, he turned and started, then frowned. "What are you doing here?"

"I need to talk to you," Matt replied.

"About what?" Bud leaned down and grabbed another couple of nails from a box on the plywood floor.

"About Miranda Harris and Carolyn Cox."

Bud sat on the top of a five-gallon pail of unopened paint and set his hammer on the floor next to him. "What about them?"

"Word around town is that you had a little thing for Miranda Harris."

Bud offered him a humorless smile. "Word around town is that I have a little thing for every single woman under the age of forty." He shrugged. "Miranda was new in town. She was pretty hot and she was single. Sure, I was interested in her, but I sure as hell didn't kill her."

"Where were you the morning she was murdered?"

Bud frowned. "I heard she was murdered like at around five or six in the morning. I would have been in bed."

"Anyone in bed with you that morning?"

"There hasn't been anybody in my bed for the last couple of months, but don't pass around that information. I've got a reputation to uphold."

There was no question, Matt didn't like Bud, but he

couldn't let his personal feelings toward the man sway his judgment.

"What about your relationship to Carolyn Cox?" Matt asked.

"What relationship?" Bud asked with a defiant lift to his chin. "I didn't have anything to do with Carolyn. She had a boyfriend."

There was something about Bud's demeanor, a rapid blink of his eyes, a slightly higher pitch to his tone, that made Matt believe there was more to the story. "Bud, come clean with me now because if something comes out later that you didn't tell me, it isn't going to look good for you."

Bud frowned. "Okay, last week I was at Carolyn's house. She called me to come over and look at her back porch which was falling down, wanted me to give her a bid on building a new one. But that's the last time I saw her. I didn't have anything to do with those murders." He got up from his makeshift seat and grabbed his hammer. "We done here? I've got work to do and time is money."

"Bud, I highly recommend that you don't leave town until these murders have been solved."

"I'm not running anywhere. I got no reason to run," he replied and then turned his back on Matt and began to bang in another nail.

Carrie was nowhere in sight as Matt left the house, a vague sense of dissatisfaction gnawing at him. Leroy,

Bud and Doc Johnson had all expressed interest in Miranda Harris.

Leroy would have had interaction with both women at the café and now Matt knew Bud had interacted with both women just days before their murders. Neither of them had alibis that could be substantiated, therefore neither of them could be removed from the short list of suspects.

As he pulled away from the Jeffers' home he could only hope that the rest of the day yielded something more productive. There had been only three days between the two murders. If the killer kept to that same time line, then he had less than forty-eight hours to find him before he struck again.

Chapter Five

It was just after noon when Jenna tore the bright yellow crime scene tape off the door and inserted her key into the lock of Miranda's house.

Now it was her house. She'd met with the lawyer, who had given her the key and gone over the terms of the will. Unlike many young women her age, Miranda had prepared for the event of her death. Jenna had signed paperwork and it was just a matter of time before it was official.

As she stepped inside the entry a new wave of grief swept through her, blowing like a hollow wind with memories of Miranda.

Jenna had always felt alone, but now her feeling of being utterly alone in the world was far more intense. Miranda had been the person who had kept her grounded, who had reminded her that there was good in the world.

She left her suitcase on the floor just inside the

doorway and went into the living room and sank down on the sofa, for a moment just breathing in the essence of the friend—the sister she had lost.

As an FBI profiler she'd worked many heinous crimes over the course of her career, but this was the first that had touched her personally. Never had she wanted to catch a killer like she wanted to catch this one.

She wasn't sure how long she sat there indulging in memories that brought both tears and laughter, but eventually she roused herself, grabbed her suitcase and went down the hallway.

Thankfully the door to the master bedroom was closed. Eventually she'd need to go in there and begin the process of packing up Miranda's things, but not today.

The guest room was across the hall from the bathroom. It was a small room decorated in bright yellow. Jenna set her suitcase on the bed and opened it. It took her only minutes to unpack the clothing she'd brought.

She hung her blouses, folded her jeans into a drawer and then stored the suitcase in the bottom of the closet. It felt as much like home as the Kansas City apartment she was rarely in.

The bathroom across the hall was decorated with a seashell motif in sea-foam greens and corals. A clamshell held a bar of soap on the sink counter and a smiling seahorse stood sentry next to it. Miranda had loved the whimsical side of life and it showed in the furnishings she had chosen.

Jenna stored her toiletries beneath the sink and wondered if there was a local charity in town. There was no point in storing Miranda's things. A charity might as well be the recipient of all her items.

Except that ugly painting. A pain stabbed Jenna's heart. The painting would leave with her and would hang wherever she lived for the rest of her life, a tangible memory of Miranda's life.

She carried her laptop and her notepad into the kitchen and set it up on the table. Matt knew this town and its people far better than she did and she trusted that he was out pounding the pavement and chasing down leads. The best thing she could do at the moment was put her thoughts and impressions down on paper and try to come up with a concrete profile of the killer.

Even though she didn't have copies of the official files in front of her, what she'd seen by reading them earlier that morning was emblazoned in her brain.

She found a can of coffee and made a pot, then finally settled in at the table with a fresh cup to do what she did best—get into the head of a criminal. To do that she had to go to dark places, fantasize what it was like for the killer as he went about his work.

Before she got down to business she sipped her

coffee and stared out the window and thought about the kiss she'd shared with Matt.

It had been hot. It had been exciting and she'd definitely wanted more. Oh, she didn't want his heart or soul. She didn't want to move in with him and make babies. She just wanted an hour of pleasure with him.

She'd warned him off. She'd told him the truth when she'd said that she didn't do relationships. So, if he decided to pursue her she wouldn't feel as bad if or when she broke his heart.

"Someday you're going to have to trust somebody," Jack Columbus, her last lover, had told her as he'd walked out of her life. "Maybe it's your job, Jenna, but you focus on finding the bad in people and you hold back big pieces of yourself. That's not how you have a meaningful relationship."

That had been a year ago and she hadn't attempted any kind of relationship since then. She told herself she was most comfortable alone, dependant on nobody, wanting nobody. But there were moments in a restaurant when she watched a family interacting with one other, or in a park when she saw a mother pushing a baby carriage, when she felt a yearning for something more.

With a frown she focused on the task at hand. She didn't have time to ruminate on how hot the sheriff was in this town. She had a killer to catch.

She began to write down random thoughts and impressions, making a list of identifying behavior patterns that had emerged at each scene.

Red roses, the traditional flower of love and romance. Both women had been stabbed through the heart. So, was the killer a spurned lover? Somebody who had loved them but had murdered them because they didn't love him back? It was definitely a likely scenario.

She powered up her laptop and got online, searching for any references to red roses. She learned that in Greek and Roman mythology the red rose was tied to the goddess of love, that early in history it became a symbol for life and deep emotion and that in today's society a rose bouquet was often the signal of the beginning of romantic intentions. But she found no reference, literary or otherwise, that might indicate what the roses meant to the killer.

She considered calling her buddy Sam to see if he could add anything off the top of his head as to what the roses might mean, but she dismissed the idea. Sam wasn't a rose kind of man. She doubted if Sam had ever given a woman flowers in his life.

Matt was more the kind of man who might give flowers to a woman he loved. Although initially he'd come at her hard, with those gray eyes of his as cold and hard as ice, she sensed a softness in him that was vastly appealing.

She frowned and focused back on her work. She couldn't just sit around and ruminate over a man just because he'd kissed her. *But what a kiss it had been,* a little voice whispered in her head.

She didn't know how long she'd been sitting at the table, jotting down notes when she felt it—a slight stir in the air, a vague feeling that she was no longer alone in the house.

Her heart leaped in her throat as she realized her gun was in her purse and her purse was on the bed in the guest bedroom.

Foolish. Foolish! She mentally reproved herself. She should have carried her gun in here, but she'd had a false sense of security in the house.

For a moment she remained seated at the table, waiting for the sensation to pass, wondering if she was just imagining things. But an overactive imagination wasn't one of Jenna's flaws and the sensation wasn't passing; instead it was growing stronger.

Soundlessly, she eased back from the table and stood, the bang of her own heartbeat almost deafening in her ears. Silently she moved to a row of kitchen drawers, seeking a weapon she could use to defend herself.

The first drawer was filled with colorful dish towels and hot pads. The second contained simple dinnerware. It was the third drawer she pulled open that gave her what she needed, a long stainless steel butcher knife that gleamed with sharpness.

She gripped it tightly in her hand and then moved quietly out of the kitchen. The living room looked just as it had when she'd entered the house, nothing out of place, nothing to indicate that anyone had come inside.

Had it been nothing more than her imagination? Were these murders getting to her in a way that none had before? She'd been thinking about the killer moments before. Was it attempting to enter the mind of the murderer that caused this crazy feeling?

As she glanced toward the front door, she saw that it was slightly ajar. An intense chill washed over her. Had she left it open when she'd carried in her suitcase? She couldn't remember.

Or had somebody come in after her?

Glancing down the hallway, her stomach clenched with nerves. Was somebody in one of the rooms? Perhaps the killer returned to the scene of the crime?

Was he waiting for her? Intending to get her before she could get him? She remembered standing outside her motel room and feeling as if somebody was watching her. Was the same person inside the house now?

She checked the bathroom first and found it empty, then slid into the guest bedroom and immediately grabbed the gun from her purse. With its solid weight in her hands she immediately felt a little bit better. She slid open the closet in that room and checked to make sure it was empty.

With the gun in one hand and the knife in the other, she stared at the closed door to the master bedroom. Her hands were slightly sweaty as nerves jangled inside her.

She could have sworn she felt the displacement of air, as if a door or window had suddenly been opened. Was somebody in the room of death, unaware that she was in the house? How could he have not known she was here? Her rental car was parked in the driveway.

Maybe it was some kind of an ambush. He was just on the other side of the door, waiting for her to enter, waiting to take her out.

Setting the knife down against the wall just outside the door, she reached out a trembling hand and grabbed the doorknob.

She held her breath as she twisted the knob and shoved the door open. Instantly she went into a shooter stance, the gun held in both hands in front of her.

She hadn't realized she was holding her breath until it whooshed out of her. There was nobody in the room, but the window was open and the screen was missing. If there had been anyone in the room he wasn't there now.

With her heart still pounding with elevated adrenaline, she raced into the hallway and out the front door. She skirted the side of the house with her gun at the ready and went around to the back.

Nobody.

There was nobody running away, no sign of anyone in the general vicinity. The adrenaline that had flooded through her slowly ebbed away as she checked the area around the open window.

The ground was too hard and the grass too short and

dry to show any footprints. She checked her watch. It was almost time for her to meet Matt at the café. She'd tell him about this and get somebody over to finger-print the windowsill, but she doubted they'd be able to lift any prints.

She returned to the house and closed the window and locked it, then grabbed her purse and left the house. As she drove toward the café another chill whispered through her.

Who had been inside the house? Was he coming after her next?

Chapter Six

Matt sat at a table in the back of the café, waiting for Jenna to arrive. Apparently Leroy's story about working twelve hours a day hadn't exactly been true because Sally the waitress had told him neither Michael, the owner, nor Leroy were working the dinner shift that night.

It had been a day of frustration. He and his deputies had interviewed anyone who might have personal information pertaining to Carolyn Cox. Just as with Miranda, none of her friends or family could imagine anyone wanting to hurt Carolyn.

According to those family members and friends, George had been a loving, devoted boyfriend and there had been no issues between them.

Two women who apparently had no enemies were dead and he was no closer to finding their killer than he'd been the day before.

He felt slightly guilty, taking time out to eat when

there was a murderer walking the streets, but the truth of the matter was he'd skipped lunch and needed to take a few minutes to not only nourish his body, but also rest his overworked mind.

He hadn't slept well the night before. Bloody red roses and dead women's faces had haunted his dreams. Tonight he had a feeling his dreams would be haunted by much different images—like that hot kiss he'd shared with Jenna.

In the moments throughout the day when his head hadn't been filled with death, it had definitely been overflowing with lust.

At that moment the object of his lust walked through the door and spotted him. As she approached he noticed that she walked with a no-nonsense stride, like a woman with a purpose, but her gaze slid left and right as if checking out everyone who was in her immediate world.

He was surprised that the mere sight of her lifted his spirits. Funny how quickly she'd gone from a pain in his butt to somebody he wanted to know better.

She sat in the chair opposite him and cast him a quick smile. "You might want to get somebody over to Miranda's house to fingerprint the back bedroom window."

"Why?"

"I think somebody came in to visit while I was there today," she replied.

"What?" He looked at her in alarm.

As she explained what had happened, a new uneasiness swept through Matt. Had the killer returned to the scene of the crime and been surprised by Jenna's presence there? But how was that possible with her car parked in front of the house?

"I guess it's possible somebody came in sometime yesterday," she continued. "I mean, I didn't hear anyone before I discovered the open window. I just got the sensation that I wasn't alone in the house, but it might have been my imagination working overtime." She picked up her water glass and took a sip.

"Do you suffer from an overactive imagination normally?" he asked.

She smiled wryly. "Never."

Matt frowned and stared at her. "Both of our victims were brunettes with blue eyes, just like you."

"Could be the beginning of a pattern or it could just be coincidence that the two women looked a lot alike," she noted. "Besides, I'm not worried. I'm an FBI agent with both a keen sense of forewarning and a gun. It's possible some teenager or curious lookie-loo decided to break in and gawk at a real murder scene."

"Maybe," he replied grudgingly.

At that moment Sally arrived at the table to take their orders. As they waited for their meals Matt filled her in on what he'd done throughout the day. "It all adds up to a big fat nothing," he said with a touch of frustration.

"Welcome to my world," she said drily. "At least we now know that Bud Carlson had contact with both women in the week before their deaths. He fits the initial profile, too."

"Initial profile?" Matt looked at her curiously.

"Generally speaking, serial killers kill within their race, so we know we're probably looking for a white male between the ages of twenty-one and thirty-five. Because he appears to be organized we can surmise that he's above average in intelligence."

"That might kick Bud off our suspect list," Matt said with a small grin.

She returned the smile. "Don't be too sure. You can be smart and still be a jerk. We know that Bud considers himself something of a ladies' man. I got the feeling the roses weren't placed on our victims' chests as burial flowers, but rather as a weird romantic gesture and as far as I'm concerned that puts our ladies' man right back on the list."

Michael Brown came through the front door and waved at Matt and Jenna. Matt offered the big man a smile as he approached their table.

"You two are quickly becoming my best customers," he said.

"I've always been one of your best customers," Matt replied. "I not only hate to cook, but I also hate to eat alone and I can always find a friend or neighbor in here."

"Everyone in town eventually sits at one of my tables," Michael exclaimed. "Is Sally taking care of both of you?"

Matt nodded. "We're good. Thanks."

"What's his story?" Jenna asked as Michael disappeared back into the kitchen.

"Homegrown, thought he was going to have a career as a professional football player but didn't make the cut. He bought this place a couple of years ago and makes the best pies I've ever tasted."

"Married?"

"No. I don't even remember him dating much."

"And Leroy, what do you know about him?"

Matt shook his head. "Not much. He's Michael's sister's kid. She moved to Chicago right out of high school and met and married her husband there. According to Michael, Leroy was having some financial trouble and so he invited him out here to take some stress off his sister."

"You might want to run a background check on him, find out if he had any other kind of trouble before coming here."

He nodded. "Already in the process."

"What have you learned about Doc Johnson? Did he have any real connection to Carolyn Cox?"

"Nothing that I have been able to substantiate, but one of Carolyn's friends said she was thinking about getting a dog."

"Which means she might have talked to the local vet about it," Jenna replied.

At that moment Sally arrived with their orders. "That's enough shoptalk for the moment," Matt said. "Talking about murder while I eat always gives me indigestion."

"I'm not sure I'm good at talking about much of anything else," she replied.

"You mentioned that the Harris family fostered you. What happened to your parents?" he asked.

She picked up her fork and raced the tines through a mound of mashed potatoes. "I never knew my father and Erika, my mother, had the maternal instincts of a rock." She paused and took a bite of the potatoes.

"I was about six when I realized we didn't live like other people did," she continued after taking a drink of her water. "Erika was a dope dealer and our little rental house was the local shooting gallery and flophouse. I was seven when I started to sleep with a knife under my pillow and I was twelve when she was arrested and sent to prison. I got lucky with the Harris family."

Although she'd told her story with little inflection, as if it were no more important than a weather forecast, Matt was appalled and could only imagine what she'd been through as a young child.

"It must have been a little tough, making the transition from that kind of lifestyle to a normal, supportive one," he said.

She gave a humorless laugh. "You can take the kid off the street, but it takes a long time to take the street off the kid. On the first night that they brought me into their home, I sneaked into the kitchen and grabbed a butcher knife to keep under my pillow. Each week Emma Harris would change the sheets on my bed and slip the knife back under my pillow. She never asked me about it, never tried to take it away from me."

"How long did you keep it there?" he asked. His heart ached for her, but he instinctively knew that if she sensed any pity from him, she'd shut down and wouldn't share anything else.

"Six months." She cut her chicken fried steak into bite-size pieces, for a moment breaking eye contact with him.

He wondered where her thoughts were taking her at the moment and suspected it wasn't a good place, but when she looked back at him her eyes were clear and untroubled.

"I just woke up one morning and knew I didn't need the knife anymore. When I'd been with them a year they wanted to adopt me, but my mother, who we knew wasn't going to get out of prison for a very long time, refused to sign away her rights. It would have been the only loving thing she could have done for me and she refused to do it. She died in prison when I turned eighteen."

It was no wonder she'd indicated she didn't do

personal relationships. The person who should have taught her about love, about trust had definitely failed at the job.

"What happened to your foster parents?" he asked.

"Miranda and I had just graduated from college when they were killed by a drunk driver."

There was a lightness in her tone that Matt thought hid a wealth of pain. Although as far as he knew she'd only grieved briefly for Miranda, he now understood more clearly the depth of her loss.

"I'm sorry," he said, knowing the words were inadequate.

She shrugged. "Stuff happens. I'll bet you had a great childhood and I'd also bet that you aren't an only child."

He looked at her in surprise. "You're right, but how would you know that? I haven't mentioned any of my siblings."

She smiled. "You mentioned that you hate to eat alone. I would guess that comes from many nights of family meals around a big table with lots of lively conversations."

"Maybe there is something to this profiling stuff," he said with a grin. "I have two sisters, both younger than me and both of them no longer living here in town. My parents moved into a retirement community in Florida two years ago. And yes, I had a good childhood."

"How did you get your scar?"

He raised a hand and touched the ridge of skin that raced down the side of his face. "Long story for another time," he said. "We'd better finish eating, then I'll go back to Miranda's with you and take a look at that window."

For the next twenty minutes they focused on their meal and small talked. Sitting across from her and watching her eat, Matt found himself remembering the kiss they had shared.

He wanted a repeat. Hearing about her past had only stirred a renewed desire for her. He wanted to fill her eyes with pleasure, hold her like she'd never been held before. He knew there was no happily-ever-after here, but for the first time in years he wanted a happily-for-a-while.

When the meal was finished, he got into his car and followed hers back to Miranda's house. As she unlocked the front door, he walked around to the back to check out the area around the window.

The screen leaned against the side of the house, one edge bent as if it had been pried off. Why would anyone take the risk of entering the house with Miranda's car parked in the driveway? With her inside the house?

He didn't understand it and what he didn't understand concerned him. Was it the work of kids, maybe entering the house on a dare? Or was it something more insidious? Had the killer returned with a new victim in his sight, Jenna with the lush brown hair and shining blue eyes?

WHILE MATT WAS OUTSIDE attempting to lift prints off the window sill, Jenna stood in the bedroom where Miranda had been murdered and looked around to see if anything in the room had been disturbed.

It didn't appear that anything had been moved or touched and if it hadn't been for the open window and removed screen, Jenna would have chalked her feeling up to a crazy burst of uncharacteristic wild imagination.

She left the bedroom and went into the kitchen where she put on a pot of coffee. It had just finished brewing when Matt came into the kitchen.

"Whoever was out there didn't leave behind any prints," he said as he pulled out a chair and sat at the table. "I suppose it's possible that the intruder approached the house from the back and didn't see your car in the driveway, didn't know you were inside."

"That makes as much sense as anything," she replied. "Want a cup of coffee?"

"Sure, sounds good." He pointed to the notebook on the table. "That reminds me, I've got copies of everything we have related to Miranda and Carolyn's murders in my car. Why don't I run out and get them."

"Thanks, I'd appreciate it."

It took him only minutes and when he was once again seated at the table she set a mug of coffee in front of him, then joined him with a mug of her own. "I think maybe tomorrow I'll meander into the local vet's office and have a little chat with the doctor."

He frowned in obvious displeasure, but before he could say anything she continued. "Matt, we have only three viable suspects right now. Leroy, Bud and Doc Johnson. To be honest, I'm not sure Leroy is bright enough to have committed these crimes and I won't be satisfied until I personally talk to both Bud and Dr. Johnson."

"Then I'd like to go with you," he replied.

She shook her head. "That would be counter-productive. It's been my experience that people are more open to chatting with women. They might tell me something that they'd never tell you."

"I don't like you putting yourself out there like that."

"Matt, I don't just sit at a desk and read reports in my duties as a special agent for the FBI. I do field-work. I interview suspects, I get my hands dirty. I'm perfectly capable of interviewing a couple of suspects without putting myself in danger."

He took a sip of his coffee, his gaze not leaving her. He lowered his cup and offered her a small smile. "I guess it's not fair of me to ask for your help and then limit your movements in the investigation."

"You're right. That wouldn't be fair." That smile of his warmed her, made her want him.

She wasn't one to fall into the sack with a man indiscriminately, but she definitely wanted Matt Buchannan like she couldn't remember wanting a man for a very long time.

She had a feeling that part of her attraction to him was because, despite the fact that they were investigating heinous crimes, she sensed a natural optimism in him, a brightness of spirit that drew her.

And there was no reason why she couldn't follow up on her attraction to him. She knew he wanted her. She'd felt the heat of his gaze lingering on her throughout dinner, remembered the taste of passion that had been on his lips when he'd kissed her.

She wasn't worried about getting drawn into anything she couldn't handle. She'd never been in a relationship where she felt at risk. She simply didn't allow it.

"What are you thinking about?" he asked, pulling her from her thoughts.

"This and that," she replied, unwilling to share these intimate thoughts with him. "You know if our killer is on the escalated time line that the first two murders indicated, then you might have another body on your hands within the next twenty-four hours."

"Don't remind me," he said with a frown. "It would help if we could find out where those roses came from."

"Or exactly what they mean to the killer," she replied, more comfortable with thoughts of the bad guy than her previous thoughts about Matt.

"We're still conducting interviews with friends and family members of both victims."

"What about putting tails on our three leading suspects?" she asked.

"I don't have the manpower or the budget to do that. Besides, the last thing I need is legal action by an innocent man for police harassment. In the meantime, I keep digging and remember that just because we have three men in our sights, it doesn't mean the guilty is on that short list."

"Miranda would have met a lot of people as a waitress at the café," Jenna said.

"So would have Carolyn as a dental assistant in the only dental office in town, and Carolyn often ate lunch at the café. So basically, anyone in town is a potential suspect at this point in time." He released a disheartened sigh.

Although Jenna was normally not a toucher, she couldn't help the impulse that led her to reach across the table and cover his hand with hers. "You'll catch him, Matt. You're smart and I have all the confidence in the world that eventually you'll get him."

"I just hope it's before another body turns up." He twined his fingers with hers. "You know, for a woman I wanted to throw into jail the first time I met her, you're definitely growing on me, Agent Taylor."

Once again she felt a flicker of heat ignite in the pit of her stomach but tried to ignore it. "I told you all about myself before we ate, now I think it's time you tell me all about you. How did you get your scar?"

He reached up and touched his face, his fingers dancing across the scar as if feeling it for the very first time. "I got it on the day my wife was murdered."

She heard the small gasp that escaped her. His wife was murdered. It was the last thing she'd expected, that he'd been that intimate with violence, with senseless tragedy. "What happened?" she asked.

He leaned back in his chair and wrapped his hands around his coffee mug. "We had a good life. I liked my job as a Chicago cop and Natalie loved her job as a social worker for Child Protective Services. We'd started talking about planning a family and things were going well."

He paused and took a sip of his coffee and his eyes darkened. He set the mug back on the table and cast his gaze out the window. "The call came in at three minutes after two on a Wednesday afternoon, a man with a gun holding hostages in the Child Protective Services office building. I got there as quickly as I could. I managed to get there before SWAT, before the brass. It was just me and a couple of patrolmen."

He turned and looked back at her. "The situation was volatile. The gunman was shooting out the window, threatening to kill the hostages one at a time. When he winged a cop I knew there wasn't time to waste. I went around the building and found an open window on the first floor. I got inside and headed for the lobby. My wife was seated on the floor, along with a dozen other people, and the gunman stood at the window screaming to the cops outside. He had a gun in one hand and a knife in the other, but all I knew was that I had to get him down. I was afraid to use my gun. The lobby was tiny and there were too many people inside for me to be comfortable with that."

He got up from the table and carried his mug to the coffeepot. He turned his back on her to refill it, then turned back to face her once again.

"I took him down and in the process he managed to cut my face. Unfortunately he also managed to squeeze off one shot before I got him on the ground."

Jenna's heart squeezed tight in her chest. "And that bullet found your wife," she said softly.

He nodded. "She died instantly. I was heralded as a hero who saved the lives of all the other people, but the price was definitely high."

Jenna didn't know what to do with her emotions. She'd never felt this kind of a heartache for another person. She got up from the table and approached him, her heart beating with the pain of his loss.

She placed a hand along the scar on the side of his face and gazed up at him. "I'm so sorry for your loss."

He put his hand over hers and for a long moment they simply gazed at one another. She felt as if they were surrounded by death, two dead women crying out for justice and another who had been loved and lost.

Jenna wanted life—right now, with him and as she raised up on her toes, she saw the white hot flame that lit his eyes.

He took her mouth, stealing her breath with the voraciousness of the kiss. His arms wrapped her up and pulled her tight against him, so tight she could tell that he was aroused.

She wrapped her arms around his neck and molded herself to him, wanting to get lost in the moment, lost in the man. Opening her mouth to him, she not only allowed him access to deepen the kiss, but rather deepened it herself, sliding her tongue into his mouth as a low moan escaped her.

He backed her up against the counter and her heart began a rapid stutter-step of pure desire. As his hands swept down the length of her back and cupped her buttocks, their kiss continued wild and hot.

It was as if nothing mattered more at the moment than the sweet sensations of being in each other's arms, of tasting each other's lips.

As he pulled her hips against his, he released a moan that stoked the flames of desire even higher inside her. She wanted him. She wanted him now.

She broke the kiss and pulled back from him. Instantly he dropped his hands from around her. "I want you, Matt."

She didn't think his gaze could grow any hotter, but it did, sliding slowly down the length of her. "I want you, too."

She reached out and took his hand and led him from the kitchen down the hallway to the guest room. Her heart kept up its rapid beat of anticipation as they entered the room and she stepped back into his embrace.

He wasn't just hot, he was also a nice man and she suddenly felt the need to warn him, to remind he was nothing but a temporary fix, a man simply for the moment.

"This has nothing to do with love," she said. "Consider me a ship passing in the night."

"And I'm any port in the storm," he replied as he reached up and dragged a finger across her lower lip. "Don't worry. No expectations," he said just before he took her mouth with his once again.

The kiss electrified her, shooting sizzling sensations down to her very toes. As the kiss continued she reached up and began to unfasten the buttons of his shirt. She wanted his warm bare skin against hers and she wanted his hot breath against her bare body.

She made short order of the buttons and he shrugged the shirt off his shoulders, exposing a tanned muscular chest and taut biceps.

He reached out and grabbed her by the bottom of her T-shirt and tugged her closer, then in one smooth movement pulled the T-shirt up and over her head.

Her nipples hardened and she wasn't sure if it was because of the coolness of the room or the heat of his gaze.

Or it might have been how his breath caught and released on a deep sigh of want that stirred her nearly mindless with desire.

As his fingers moved to the fastening of his slacks, she unbuttoned her jeans, sat on the bed and pulled them off. By the time she'd finished he stood before her in a pair of briefs that strained against his arousal.

Instead of desire she saw a wave of panic cross his features. "I don't have any protection," he said.

There was no way Jenna was going to allow this moment to explode apart. "I'm on the Pill and I trust you if you trust me." She held her breath to see what happened next. He'd subtly indicated that he hadn't been with a woman since the death of his wife, but he knew very little about her sexual history.

She couldn't blame him if he pulled his pants on and walked out, but sweet anticipation winged through her as he stepped closer and pulled her into his arms.

He kissed her ravenously, as if she tasted better than anything he'd ever had in his life and with their lips still locked they tumbled onto the bed.

It was as if she'd been ready for him forever. Within minutes they were naked together, stroking heated flesh and exploring the secrets of each other.

As his hands cupped her breasts and his mouth found

one of her nipples, she couldn't help the low moan that escaped her lips. She tangled her hands in his hair, loving the feel of the rich soft strands against her skin.

His long hardness pressed against her thigh, the feel of it sending her surprisingly close to climax. When his hands moved down the length of her body and his fingers touched the core of her, the wave washed over her hard and fast and she cried out in stunned surprise at the intensity.

Immediately he positioned himself between her thighs. She was more than ready for him and welcomed him by opening her legs.

As he entered her his gaze locked with hers, his eyes shining silver in the deep glow of twilight that filled the room.

She closed her eyes, finding his gaze even more intimate than their act of lovemaking. As he began to stroke deep and slow within her, she felt the rising tide begin to sweep over her again. She clung to him as reality filtered away and thought became impossible. There was only Matt and this moment and she gave herself to it as she was swept over the edge.

He stiffened against her and groaned her name as he found his own release. For a moment neither of them moved, then he shifted the bulk of his weight to her side and tenderly kissed her forehead.

In that instant she wanted him gone, out of her bed

and out of this house. He felt too close, too good. He felt like danger.

Without saying a word, she scooted out of the bed and padded across the hall to the bathroom. She stared at her reflection in the mirror, the tousled hair and the swollen lips. *Don't let him in,* a little voice whispered in the back of her head. It was the same voice that had kept her safe through her miserable childhood, the same that had kept her from wanting or needing anyone in her life.

She cleaned up and pulled on her short summer bathrobe, then returned to the bedroom, disappointed to find him still in the bed. She flipped on the overhead light as darkness had fallen outside the windows.

"It's getting late. You should go," she said.

He sat up, the sheet falling to expose his magnificent chest. "Feels a little like slam, bam, thank you ma'am."

She felt a blush warm her cheeks. "I just have things to do and I'm not one to bask in the afterglow. I'll be in the kitchen."

As she left the bedroom she turned on lights in the living room and then in the kitchen. She would have liked a cup of coffee, but feared that if she made any he'd take it as an invitation to hang around and have a cup.

The files he'd brought to her sat on the table, and after the brief escape from death into his arms, she was once again eager to read the files and see if she could come up with something that might have been missed.

She turned as he came into the kitchen, his eyes

dark and unreadable as he gazed at her. "I guess I'll see you sometime tomorrow?" It was obvious from his tone that he was reluctant to leave, perhaps hesitant to leave her alone with a killer on the loose.

"I'll check in sometime tomorrow afternoon," she replied. She needed some space from him. "I'll walk you out," she said firmly.

Together they left the kitchen and headed for the front door. When they reached it he turned back to her and she felt the need to explain away what had happened between them.

"Matt, I don't normally fall into bed with a man days after I meet him. This tonight was out of the ordinary and probably shouldn't happen again."

"But if it did happen again, I wouldn't be real upset," he said with a small smile. "Good night, Jenna."

She stepped out on the porch and watched him walk to his car. She could have stayed in his arms through the dark night, could have been wrapped up in his strong embrace, with the beat of his heart against hers.

For a moment a wave of yearning swept through her, a desire for something more, for something indefinable. She wrapped her robe more tightly around her as his car drove down the street.

When the sound of his car was no longer audible, she remained standing in the moonlight, wishing things were different, wishing *she* were different.

She was just about to go inside when she felt it, the

subtle sense of no longer being alone. She'd always been good at instantly analyzing a situation for danger. She was adept at listening to her instincts, decoding her natural fear responses.

Glancing around she tried to figure out what could have possibly triggered the flood of adrenaline that worried through her, the sense of unease that whispered of danger.

Unable to figure out what had caused the feeling, she slid back through the door and locked it behind her.

SHE WAS JUST LIKE the others with her brown hair and blue eyes, with her innocent smile and wicked heart. He watched her from behind a tree across the street until she went back into the house.

He tamped down the rage that buoyed up inside him, a rage that had been born a month ago. He couldn't get to the woman who had created the rage, but he'd suddenly realized that Miranda Harris looked like the object of his hatred and when he'd played out the fantasy and she was dead, some of the rage had gone away, but not for long.

He'd thought Carolyn Cox might ease the pain that tortured him, but killing her hadn't helped either. Maybe this one would finally eradicate the burning torture of memory, quench the fiery need for revenge.

Maybe killing Jenna Taylor would finally give him peace.

Chapter Seven

Normally Jenna was out of bed by six. She was naturally an early riser and rarely slept in. But this morning it was just after seven-thirty when she pulled herself out of bed and stumbled wearily into the shower.

It had been a long night. She'd sat at the kitchen table and read over the files Matt had brought, comparing the crime scenes, looking for similarities and differences between the two murders and anything that might have been missed initially.

She'd charted and graphed and created her own little murder book but felt no closer to coming up with a concrete profile on their killer.

When she'd finally fallen in bed around three, her dreams had been haunted by blood red roses and visions of herself with a knife through her heart. Even when those nightmares had passed, she'd dreamed of Matt and in that dream he was the one wielding a knife and chasing her.

It didn't take a psychiatrist to understand the final dream. Although she knew Matt was no physical threat to her, he threatened her well-being with the power of his smile, with the fire of his kisses, with the pleasure in his touch.

He made her want things that scared her because they had the capacity to hurt her. Miranda was the only person she'd ever let into her heart and look how that had turned out.

Once she was showered and dressed, she had her day planned out. First stop, Dr. Patrick Johnson, town vet. She'd spoken to the man briefly on the night of Carolyn Cox's murder, but she wanted to talk to him alone, get a look, a feel for the man herself without the sheriff around. And after that she was hunting down Bridgewater's resident bad boy, Bud Carlson, for the same reason.

She left the house just after eight-thirty and headed for the vet's office. When she got there the hours printed on the door told her he didn't open until nine-thirty. With almost an hour to spare, she went next door into the cool comfort of the café.

Michael greeted her with his usual pleasant smile as she sat on a stool at the counter. "Breakfast?" he asked as he held a menu.

"Sure, why not?" she agreed and accepted the menu from him.

"Any progress on these crimes?" Michael asked as

he poured her a cup of coffee. Leroy sidled up next to his uncle.

"We're getting closer to identifying our perp every minute," she said, although it was a lie. The last thing she knew Matt would want the townspeople to know was just how far away they were from making an arrest.

"How come a pretty woman like you isn't married?" Michael asked.

"Never felt the need," she replied.

"Maybe she's just a love 'em and leave 'em type," Leroy quipped, then he blushed so violently the tips of his ears turned red.

"Speaking of love 'em and leave 'em," Michael said beneath his breath as he looked over Jenna's shoulder to the young man who had just entered the café.

She sat up straighter on the stool as he approached them and slid onto the stool next to hers. Perfect. He'd made it easy for her.

"Morning, Bud," Michael said. "The usual?"

"Yeah, and plenty of coffee," Bud replied. "And don't give me a cup of that crap that's been sitting in the pot for hours."

"What about you, Jenna. Have you made up your mind?" Michael asked.

"I'll have the breakfast special," she replied and handed him back the menu.

Leroy left the counter as Michael poured Bud a cup of coffee, then Michael disappeared into the kitchen.

"You're that FBI lady, aren't you?" Bud asked.

Jenna turned and looked at him. Bud was a good-looking man. His dark brown hair was thick and wavy and his brown eyes snapped with a flirtatious intelligence that might have been appealing if it wasn't for the slight sneer of his upper lip.

"I'm Jenna Taylor," she said. "And you are?"

He snorted. "You know who I am. Word around town is that I'm your number one suspect."

"That's not true," she replied. "Oh, you're on the list, but at the moment almost everyone in town is on the list."

He cupped his big hands around his cup of coffee. "I shouldn't be on your list at all. I didn't have anything to do with those two women's murders."

"You know, I'm not here as an FBI agent. Miranda was my best friend. I'm just here trying to figure out what happened to her, who took her away from me." Jenna pushed for a touch of vulnerability in her tone. "I heard you liked her, that you flirted with her."

"Guilty as charged," he replied easily. "And she flirted back with me." He puffed out his chest like a big rooster about to crow. "You could say I have a way with the ladies."

"Did you go out with Miranda?"

"Nah, it never got that far. When she first got to

town I was kind of involved with somebody else." He took a sip of his coffee and then continued as he set the cup back on the counter.

"Miranda was different than the women here. She had a real class to her. I'd just worked up my nerve to ask her out when I heard about the murder." Once again his chest expanded. "She would have gone out with me, too. I could see it in her eyes when she talked to me. She liked me and she would have jumped at the chance to have a date with me. But I sure as hell didn't kill her."

Jenna wasn't sure if she believed him or not. Bud was easy to profile, a man with a lack of self-esteem who compensated with a swaggering bravado. The fact that he mentioned that Miranda was different, that she was classy, intrigued her.

Was it possible that secretly Bud had thought Miranda felt she was too good for him? Had that stirred up a rage inside him?

At that moment Leroy came out of the kitchen with their breakfast plates in hand. Jenna's special consisted of two eggs, two strips of bacon and toast. Bud's usual was a tall stack of pancakes with sausage links. Leroy set down the plates and then once again disappeared into the kitchen.

"From what I understand, Miranda was pretty popular. I heard that Leroy had a crush on her."

Bud laughed. "That man has a crush on anybody

who is nice to him and doesn't smell like bacon grease." His smile fell as he lowered his voice. "The guy is weird. If he isn't on your suspect list, then he should be."

"What about Doc Johnson?"

Bud looked at her in surprise. "What about him?"

"I heard he had a thing for Miranda."

"I wouldn't know anything about that. Patrick and I don't exactly run in the same circles," Bud said with a scowl. "He was an asshole when he was sweeping the floors in his daddy's car dealership and as far as I'm concerned, he's an asshole with his fancy degree that put a Dr. in front of his name."

He leaned toward her, his eyes holding a blatant flirtatious light. "Now, tell me about Jenna Taylor. Are you having any fun while you've been in town? I'd be glad to show you around. You know, take you to all the hot spots."

"I didn't know there were hot spots in Bridgewater," she replied.

He grinned. "My place is one of the hottest."

At that moment Michael returned to the counter with the coffeepot in hand. He scowled at Bud. "You harassing my customers?"

"He's all right," Jenna replied. "And thanks for the offer, Bud, but I'm only in town for a couple of days and besides, you just aren't my type."

Michael snorted back a burst of laughter as Bud's

eyes sparked with anger. "Guess that put you in your place," Michael exclaimed as he topped off Bud's cup.

"She doesn't know what she's missing," he replied and once again looked at Jenna. "Sometimes a walk on the wild side is just what a woman needs."

Bud didn't speak to her again and Jenna was left wondering how wild his wild side might be. Wild enough to give a woman roses, then stab her through the heart?

She'd ticked him off on purpose to see what kind of a response he'd give her. It was kind of like poking a dangerous bear with a stick to see what it would do.

Bud left the café before Jenna and when she stepped outside into the hot morning air she thought about how she'd approach her next interview.

The door to Dr. Patrick Johnson's office opened with a tinkle of a bell and Jenna entered to be greeted by a smiling receptionist.

"I was wondering if I could speak with Dr. Johnson," Jenna said.

"Why don't you have a seat and I'll see if he's available," the young woman replied.

Jenna was seated on one of the plastic chairs for only a moment before the inner door opened and a tall, attractive blond man gestured her inside.

"Agent Taylor," he said as he held out a hand to her.

"Jenna, please make it Jenna," she said. He had a firm handshake and when it ended his blue eyes regarded her curiously.

"What can I do for you, Jenna Taylor?"

"I was wondering if I could speak to you about Miranda Harris."

His eyes clouded with sadness and he gestured her into an office where he sat behind the desk and she sat in the chair in front of him.

"Miranda was a lovely woman and what happened to her is a real tragedy," he said as he leaned back in his big leather chair. "But you and Matt already spoke to me about all this."

Jenna nodded. "I just thought you might have thought of something else that could be helpful in the investigation. Word around town is that you showed a definite interest in Miranda."

"Why wouldn't I have been interested? She was bright and beautiful and funny. For the first time in years I looked forward to going into the café knowing I was going to see her smile."

"But you never asked her out?" Jenna asked.

"I was taking things slow. I was coming off a bad relationship and didn't want to make mistakes." He straightened his desk blotter and moved a pen to align perfectly with it.

When he looked at Jenna again his gaze was filled with remorse. "I keep thinking that maybe if I'd asked her out, if we'd become a couple, then she wouldn't have been murdered. I know it's crazy but I feel partly responsible for her death."

He cleared his throat and ran a hand down the front of his white coat as if to erase an invisible wrinkle. "If you've come here looking for answers, I'm afraid I don't have any to give to you. I can't imagine who did this, I can't imagine anyone wanting to hurt her."

He might not have thought that he'd told Jenna anything substantial, but he'd definitely given her little clues to his personality.

"You said you'd had a relationship that ended badly. What does that mean?" she asked.

A small hint of color filled his cheeks. "Is there nothing off limits?"

"Not in a murder investigation," she replied.

"It's no deep, dark secret. I was in love, she wasn't. End of story."

"What was her name?"

"June Alexander, not that it matters. She moved away and I have no idea where she went." The warmth of his eyes had faded, replaced by a faint chill as a yapping bark came from the reception area. "Are we done here? My next patient has arrived."

"Thank you for talking to me," she said as she stood. "As Miranda's best friend I'm just trying to make sense of this."

The chill in his eyes warmed once again. "There is no sense to it, and I'm sorry for your loss. I find it difficult to go into the café now. I'll miss seeing that smile of hers."

Jenna saw herself out into the lobby where an older woman held a yappy dog no bigger than her purse in her lap. Jenna offered the woman a faint smile as she left the office, her mind whirling with the information she'd gleaned.

Dr. Patrick Johnson was a perfectionist, highly organized and intelligent. He would have had the mental tools to pull off the crimes and there was obviously a painful romance in his recent past.

She definitely wanted to find out about June Alexander. It was amazing how quickly a simple question could yield information that led to another question in a murder investigation. Most of the time there were short forays on wild goose chases, a head butt against a dead end, but nothing could be left to chance.

Too many criminals had been caught by the wisp of a lead that didn't appear promising, by an investigator following what appeared to be a dead end.

She got into her car and stuck the key into the ignition. The next stop was the sheriff's office where she'd check in with Matt.

Matt. She didn't like the way her heart sang his name. She'd known the man for only three days and had already slept with him, had already told him about her childhood.

She'd already been more intimate with him than she'd ever been with any man. No more, she told herself. From here on out it had to remain strictly business between them. She couldn't afford to let him in any closer.

Putting the car into Reverse, she turned to look over her shoulder before backing out and that's when she saw it on the passenger seat. An icy chill shot up her back as she stared at the perfect, long-stem red rose.

"THANKS, I APPRECIATE YOUR time," Matt said into the phone, then hung up and released a sigh of frustration. He pulled his list in front of him and crossed through the name of Mark Harris. Miranda's ex-husband had a rock-solid alibi at the time of her murder. He'd been working the night shift at his job in a factory in Dallas. A call to his supervisor had confirmed that he'd been there until noon on the day of the murder. It was physically impossible for him to have been here in Bridgewater murdering his ex-wife and at work at the same time.

Even though it was just after ten, Matt already felt the burn of aggravation by his lack of progress. Two murders and not enough physical evidence left behind to fill a page. Two murders and not a viable suspect leaping to the head of the list.

And if the killer stayed on the time line he'd established between Miranda and Carolyn's murder, then by tomorrow morning there should be another body. God, he couldn't let that happen. How was he supposed to protect all the young women in his town?

There was a rapid knock on the door and Joey stuck his head inside. "Agent Taylor is here to see you," he said.

Matt couldn't help that his spirits lifted just a little bit as he anticipated Jenna's presence. He told himself it was because he hoped she was bringing something concerning their investigation, but he knew that was a lie. His pleasure in seeing her again was strictly male and had nothing to do with business.

She swept into the office with a simmering energy. Dressed in a pair of white jeans and a red short-sleeved blouse, she looked better prepared for a picnic than a murder investigation.

"Good morning," he said and gestured her toward the chair in front of his desk.

"Busy morning," she replied and ignored the chair. "You might want to grab an evidence kit and come with me outside to my car."

He sat up straighter. "Why? What's going on?"

"Come outside and you'll see."

Matt followed her outside where she pointed to the passenger-side door of her car. "Don't touch it. Just look inside."

Matt peered in through the window and his heart stuttered to a halt as he saw the red rose lying on the upholstery. "Where did that come from?" he asked as he straightened and looked at her.

"I found it there when I left Dr. Johnson's office a few minutes ago," she replied.

"Consider your car officially impounded," he said as a muscle pulsed at his jaw. "And come back inside and tell me exactly what you've been doing this morning."

When he returned to the office Joey and Abe sat at their desks. "Abe, I'm impounding Agent Taylor's rental car. I want you to go over it with a fine-tooth comb and pay particular attention to the passenger side. Joey, there's a rose on the passenger seat, see to it that it's bagged and tagged."

Joey's eyes opened wide as he looked first at Matt, then at Jenna. "Yes, sir," he said and jumped to his feet.

Matt turned to face Jenna. "In my office. I need to take a detailed statement from you."

Marked. She'd been marked by their killer. Or was it just some kind of crazy coincidence? Had some man developed a little crush on the beautiful FBI agent and left a rose in her car? Matt didn't believe in those kind of coincidences.

Once again he sat at the desk and she took the seat before him, her features composed as if she had no idea what that rose might have meant to her, to her safety.

"Tell me where you've been and what you've done this morning. How long was the car out of your sight? Did you see anyone lingering around just before you discovered the rose?"

"The rose wasn't there when I left the house this morning," she said. "I parked in front of the café and realized I was too early to speak to Dr. Johnson, so I went into the café for some breakfast. While I was there Bud Carlson came in and sat next to me at the counter."

Matt raised an eyebrow. "You talked to him?"

Her lips curved in a wry smile. "He offered to show me all the hot spots in town, starting with his place."

Matt was stunned by the unexpected wave of jealousy that swept through him. He wanted to tell her that she was his woman and should never entertain the thought of being with any other man.

He knew his reaction was totally inappropriate and consciously willed it away. "Did you leave the café first or did Bud?" he asked.

"Bud left first. I ticked him off, told him that he wasn't my type."

"Do you really think that's wise?" Matt asked with a touch of aggravation. "I mean, we're looking for a killer here and it's possible you just baited him."

She shrugged as if unconcerned at the very idea. "After I left the café I went in to speak to Dr. Johnson. Do you know what happened to June Alexander?"

Matt blinked, trying to keep up with her. "How did June come up in the conversation?"

"Patrick told me that he'd had a previous bad relationship with a woman named June Alexander. That would fit into the profile of our killer. He told me she'd left town, but I think we need to check up on her."

Matt wrote her name down to remind himself to do some follow-up. "I know most of the people in town, but I don't know all the ins and outs of their romantic lives," he said. "I knew Patrick and June had dated, but I didn't know it had ended badly."

He leaned back in his chair and looked at her. "So, Bud would have had the opportunity to put that rose into your car."

She nodded. "And so would have Patrick, or Leroy, or anyone else in town who might have walked past my car."

Matt blew a sigh of frustration and tried to ignore the hot burn of worry that tortured his stomach. She'd received a rose. The words reverberated around and around in his head, a deep echo of danger.

"You know what the rose means," he finally said. "The killer has you in his line of fire."

"One rose doesn't scare me," she replied easily. "His pattern is five roses, then death." In one of the conversations they'd had about the roses, Matt had mentioned that he believed they had been given one at a time, as they were all in progressive stages of bloom.

"But what if he breaks his pattern?" Matt asked, the burn in his stomach intensifying. The thought of anyone hurting her made him feel ill.

"He won't," she said with certainty. "The pattern is important to him, as important as the killings themselves. He needs the ritual."

"And you know this how?"

"Years of studying serial killers and a gut instinct that has never proven me wrong," she replied.

"And you're willing to bet your life on that?"

"Look at it this way, if he's targeting me, then chances are he isn't targeting any other woman."

Matt stared at her for a long moment. "You were hoping this would happen. You've been all over town, highly visible to the killer. You wanted him to target you."

"I thought there was a possibility he might," she said. "I have the same hair and eye color as Miranda and Carolyn. We all look similar, so I knew there was a chance that I could be targeted."

"We need to get you into protective custody," Matt exclaimed.

"Absolutely not," she replied with a stubborn lift of her chin. "This isn't my first time at the rodeo, cowboy. I can take care of myself and the last thing I want is for the perp to think I have backup or protection." She leaned forward, her eyes gleaming an electric blue. "I want him to come after me."

"Is this some kind of death wish that you have?"

Her cheeks flushed pink. "Of course not." She stood. "I need to get home and get on the Internet and see if I can find June Alexander. Since you have my car, can you take me home?"

Matt got up from his desk and gestured to his

computer. "Why don't you do that here and I'll go check on the progress on your car. If you hang out here for a couple of hours, then we should be through with it."

As he walked to the door, she settled into his chair. "Any info you can share with me about June Alexander that might help me find her?" she asked.

Matt frowned thoughtfully. "If I remember right, she came to town when her father died and moved into his house. She'd been living someplace back east, but I can't remember where. She went to work for Stan Martin in his stained-glass shop. You might talk to him, maybe he knows where she moved to when she left here."

What he wanted to do was bubble wrap her like a precious package and mail her to a distant state where she would be safe from the madman who now had her in his sights. He wanted to put her in a safety deposit box and lock her into a bank vault.

"I'll check back in a little while," he said and then left the office. At least for the moment she was in the safest place she could be and nobody could harm her.

He'd recognized a streak of stubbornness in her the first time he'd met her, but it worried him that she also seemed to have little or no fear.

It wasn't healthy not to be afraid. Fear was what made people cautious, that spike of fear adrenaline heightened senses and the desire for self-preservation. It was dangerous to be fearless.

The impound lot was behind the sheriff's office. It was a small chain-link area with a shed big enough to hold one car. Most vehicles were impounded due to drunk driving. At the moment there was only one vehicle on the lot and it was in the shed—Jenna's car.

He entered the shed and the hot air inside burned his lungs. Abe was dusting the passenger side of the car. When he saw Matt he shook his head. "Nothing on the inside," he said. "And it doesn't look like I'm going to pull anything up on the door handle. Whoever left that rose was very careful not to leave any prints or anything else behind."

Matt sighed in frustration as Abe continued. "I'm going to go over it all another time, but I don't think I missed anything the first time."

When Matt returned to the office Joey stood from his desk. "I've got some information on Leroy," he said.

"Let's go back into the conference room," Matt replied. The conference room had become the war room for the two murders. Three whiteboards had been hung, one holding all the information and crime scene photos for Miranda, one for Carolyn and the third a list of similarities and links between the two.

Joey sat at the table, a sheath of papers in front of him and Matt sat across from him. "What have you got?" Matt asked.

"Apparently financial troubles weren't the only

problems that Leroy had before he came here to live with his uncle. He also had problems with a woman."

"What do you mean? What kind of problems?"

"Elizabeth Walker took out a restraining order against Leroy six months before he moved here. I managed to contact her this morning and she told me that she and Leroy had dated a couple of times, but when she told him she didn't want to see him anymore, he became a stalker. She also suspects that he broke windows on her car and slashed her tires, but she couldn't prove it because she didn't see him do it."

"Interesting," Matt said as he thought of the man who'd often served his meals to him in the café.

"And get this, Elizabeth has brown hair and blue eyes," Joey exclaimed.

"How do you know that?"

"I asked her. I also asked her if Leroy liked to give her flowers, but she said he'd never given her anything." Joey looked at Matt with the eagerness of a young pup.

"Great job, Joey," Matt said. "I knew I could depend on you to do a thorough job."

Joey smiled at the compliment. "Anything else you want me to do?"

Matt leaned back in his chair pensively. Every deputy on his little force was working on the murder investigations. They were knocking on doors and talking to people about both Miranda and Carolyn, following the smallest leads that might come out of those interviews.

"Maybe you could help Jerry with the calls to the florist shops," Matt said. "It's a big job and so far he hasn't had any success locating a place that was selling six roses at a time around the dates of the murders."

"No problem," Joey replied. "I'll coordinate with him and maybe between the two of us we can break this case wide open." He jumped up from the table as if flames burned his butt and disappeared from the room.

Matt remained seated at the desk, thinking about Jenna and about the rose. She was in danger. Surely the killer must have known that in giving the rose he was also giving her warning of his intent.

Why would he give them that kind of heads-up? Why would he point a finger to his next victim? The ultimate challenge, he thought. Taking down an FBI agent would be a high like no other.

Jenna wanted to be a lone wolf, dealing with the situation on her own, but he wasn't going to allow that. She was using herself as bait and he didn't like it. He didn't like it one bit.

He needed to talk some sense into her, make her realize she could trust him to have her back. He had a feeling she was a woman who didn't trust easily. He knew enough about her background to recognize that she wasn't accustomed to having people she could trust in her life, that there had never been anyone for her to lean on.

She might be a lone wolf, but he was an alpha wolf, leader of the pack and there was no way he was going to let the hunter get to her.

Chapter Eight

Jenna hung up the phone and stared at the notes she'd taken in front of her. She'd sensed a nasty little temper in Dr. Patrick Johnson when she'd spoken to him earlier in the day and June Alexander had just confirmed it.

She'd found the woman through her Web page, advertising a stained-glass store in Houston. A call to the shop had confirmed that she was the woman who used to live in Bridgewater and had dated Patrick.

June had nothing good to say about the vet. He was controlling and obsessive, he had an explosive temper that at times had frightened her and the longer they had dated the worse those traits had gotten. When she'd finally broken up with him, she'd decided her best course of action was to relocate someplace else.

Intelligent, controlling and possessing an explosive temper; all traits that should move him back to the top of their suspect list except for the fact that June Alexander had been a blonde.

Of course it was possible something happened between the time he dated June and the present that had set him on a hatred against brunettes. Or it could still be coincidental that the two dead women had been brown haired with blue eyes.

She leaned back in the chair and caught a whiff of Matt's cologne and the familiar scent stirred her on a hundred different levels. She couldn't help but remember how it had felt to be in his arms, how his eyes had glowed with emotion as he took possession of her.

For just a moment she'd felt safe. She'd almost felt loved, and it had taken her breath away, filled her with both an indescribable yearning and a shuddering fear.

She started as the door swung open and Matt walked in, a deep scowl on his features. "Looks like our man left no fingerprints outside of the door or inside the car." He sat in the chair opposite her at his desk.

"Did you really expect him to make that kind of stupid mistake?" she asked.

"One could hope," he replied. "Have you had any luck contacting June Alexander?"

For the next few minutes she filled him in on what she'd learned about Patrick and then he told her what Joey had discovered about Leroy.

"So, the two men at the top of our short list are Leroy and Patrick," she said. "They fit the profile and nothing I've learned about them has done anything to kick them off our list." She smiled at him. "Let's put it this way, if one of them knocks on my door late at night in the next week, I'm not going to let them inside unless I have my gun in my hand."

"I want to talk to you about that," he said and leaned forward, his scowl deepening.

"Talk to me about what?"

"About staying at Miranda's house. I don't want you there."

A small laugh escaped her lips at the autocratic tone of his voice. "I don't think that's your call, Sheriff Buchannan," she replied coolly. Just because she'd slept with him didn't mean he owned her and he certainly didn't have the right to boss her around.

"When somebody is too stubborn for their own good, then it should be my call," he replied. "Jenna, I want you to stay with me, in my house."

Jenna looked at him in surprise. "I can't do that," she replied.

"Why not?" Once again he leaned forward, his gaze as intense as she'd ever seen it. "I have a big house with a nice spare bedroom. You'd be safer there than in Miranda's house all alone."

"What are you going to do? Give up the investigation to babysit me?"

"Of course not," he replied. "We could work together here and around town on the investigation, but in the evenings and through the night I could make sure you're safe."

Oh, there was seduction in his words, in his offer of safety. She could easily imagine them sharing coffee in the mornings, spending evenings together in the intimacy of his living room.

For a single shining moment she wanted what he offered, wanted it as much as anything she'd ever wanted in her life, but along with the want came the fear.

Before she could reply he stood and leaned over the desk. "Jenna, I lost one woman I cared deeply about to violence. I don't want to lose another." His voice was low and trembled slightly with emotion.

The thought of a serial killer after her didn't scare her half as much as Matt Buchannan. "I'll be okay at Miranda's," she said forcefully. "I'm a light sleeper. I'd hear anyone who might try to break in."

He straightened and blew out an audible sigh. "I know you're not used to having anyone to depend on, but you can depend on me, Jenna." His gaze seemed to pierce the armor she wore, to look deep into her very soul. "I'd never let you down."

She knew that about him. She knew the kind of man he was and that's what frightened her most. He was everything she was not—he was an optimist, a man who believed in love and the ultimate power of goodness.

"I have to do this my way, Matt," she finally said. She had to maintain her distance from him, no matter what the cost. "Trust me, I'll be careful."

She could tell her answer didn't make him happy. His lips pressed tightly together and a muscle ticked at his jaw.

"So, where do we go from here?" she asked in an attempt to break the tension.

"Why don't we go back in the conference room and I'll have some of the men update us on anything new," he replied.

She was conscious of him just behind her as she left his inner office and walked down the hallway to the conference room.

The scent of him enticed her, the confident energy that wafted from him calmed her and she wondered if she'd made a mistake in turning down his offer to stay in his house.

She reminded herself that she was a trained FBI agent and could take care of herself. She didn't need Matt taking care of her.

Morning turned into afternoon as the deputies updated their progress and then Matt and Jenna kicked around ideas and theories about the murders.

"We don't have the trigger," she said and took a sip of her third cup of coffee since a lunch of burgers that had been brought in by one of the deputies.

"If the guilty party is somebody like Patrick Johnson or Leroy or anyone else who has been in town for a while, then it would help if we knew what triggered the murders."

"Maybe it was the arrival of Miranda in town," Matt said thoughtfully.

"Possible," Jenna agreed. "She might have reminded our killer of another woman…a lover who left him, or a mother who beat him."

"But we know that June Alexander doesn't look like our victims. She had blond hair and brown eyes."

"True," Jenna agreed. "But we still can't be a hundred percent certain that he's chosen his victims based on a specific physical look. He might have chosen them based on a particular personality trait."

Matt offered her a half smile as his eyes twinkled with a touch of humor. "Doubtful. All the people we talked to about the victims said they were easy to get along with and never made anyone mad. You definitely don't fit that victim profile."

She gave him a cheeky grin. "Love me or hate me, it doesn't make any difference to me," she replied. "Besides, I'm never in one place long enough to reap the consequences of my actions." It was a reminder to herself and to him that this time in Bridgewater, Texas, was just a brief stopover, that she had a life to get back to in Kansas City.

For the rest of the afternoon they checked and double checked forensic reports and reread interviews, looking for something, anything they might have missed on the last round of reading.

It was just after six when Jenna stood and stretched

with her arms overhead. She was exhausted and felt as if they'd spent the last eight hours doing nothing but spinning their wheels.

"Are you going to release my car to me so I can drive myself home?" she asked.

He didn't meet her gaze. "We aren't quite finished with it, so I'll take you home."

She had a feeling he was telling her a white lie, that he just didn't want her driving home alone. "Then if you don't mind, I'm ready to call it a day."

"What about dinner? Do you want to grab something at the café before I take you home?" he asked.

She frowned and shook her head. "I think I've tried every special Michael has to offer and to tell the truth I'm rather sick of the café food."

"What about Mexican? We have a great little Mexican restaurant just a mile or so outside of town."

She shook her head once again. "No, thanks, I'll just open a can of soup or something at home."

"Okay, then I guess I'll take you home." It was obvious he wasn't happy with the idea. "But, I want to come inside and check all the locks on the windows and doors," he said as they left the office and walked out into the hot evening air.

"I checked them all and they're as good as locks can get," she replied.

"But somebody got into that bedroom window," he reminded her as they got into the patrol car.

"And I'm fairly sure they came through an unlocked front door. My bad," she exclaimed. "And that opportunity won't present itself to anyone again. All the doors at Miranda's house have dead bolts and I intend to use them. Besides, like I told you before, a single rose doesn't scare me. I'm confident he won't abandon his ritual for a quick kill."

"I hope you're right," Matt said.

They were silent for the remainder of the drive to Miranda's place. Once there they both got out of the car and walked to the front porch where Jenna dug the key out of her purse and then unlocked the door.

"I want to check it out before you go inside," Matt said and drew his weapon. Before she could stop him he disappeared through the door.

It felt strange, to have a man so intent on taking care of her. Sam was always ragging on her that sometimes she needed to take a step back and allow somebody to do something nice for her. She had to admit, Matt's protectiveness felt good even if she felt it was unnecessary.

He's just doing his job, she told herself, and yet she knew it was more than that. She was more than a coworker to him, more than somebody he needed to protect as a guest in his town.

I already lost one woman I cared about deeply to violence. I don't want to lose another. His words played in her mind, filling her with a curious combination of warmth and dread. She didn't want him to care about her and more importantly she didn't want to care about him.

"Satisfied?" she asked as he returned to the porch with his gun back in his holster.

"Not really. I'd rather have you locked up in my jail cell where I know you'd be safe."

"Since we both know that's not going to happen, I'll just tell you good night. You'll pick me up in the morning?"

He nodded. "How about around seven?"

"Fine. Good night, Matt."

He murmured a good-night and she closed the door, careful to lock it and throw the dead bolt. Immediately the silence of the house pressed in around her.

The entire time she'd been in Bridgewater she'd carried her gun in her purse, but now she went into the bedroom and pulled on her shoulder holster. She'd wear it until bedtime and then sleep with it beneath her pillow. Nobody was going to sneak up on her without seeing the business end of her revolver in his face.

After eating a bowl of soup, she began the arduous task of packing up some of Miranda's things in a couple of boxes she'd found in the garage.

It was a difficult task as she wrapped and boxed knick-knacks from the living room. So many of the items held not only meaning for Miranda but for Jenna as well.

There was a tacky Kewpie doll that Jenna had won for her friend by shooting at rubber ducks at a carnival they'd attended. There were framed photos of the two of them that she placed in a separate box, one that she would take with her when she left.

It was after nine when she finally decided to call it a night. Instead of sleeping in the guest room she made up her mind to bunk on the sofa for the night. She put on her nightgown and then carried her gun, a pillow and a spare blanket into the living room.

Once she was settled on the sofa with her gun on the coffee table next to her, she knew she wouldn't sleep. She was conscious of every noise the house made, the tick of a clock on the bookcases, the hum of the air conditioner through the vents, and the occasional rumble of the ice maker coming from the kitchen.

Jenna knew most people would be afraid at the prospect of a killer targeting them, but sometimes she felt as if all the fear that she was to experience for her entire life had been expended during her horrible childhood.

But as she lay there alone on the sofa with the unfamiliarity of the house, the strange sounds surrounding her, she felt an edge of fear rise up in the back of her throat.

As darkness fell outside she turned on the lamp next to the sofa, finding the night more difficult to handle than she'd thought it would be.

It was after eleven when she got up and rechecked the windows and doors. With her gun in hand she opened the front door and peered out into the yard, looking for anything that might be amiss.

She checked up the street and froze as she saw an unfamiliar sports car parked along the curb two houses away. From the faint glow of the streetlight she could tell that somebody was in the driver's seat.

She watched for several long moments but the person behind the steering wheel didn't move. Why didn't he get out of the car?

Who was it and why was he just parked there? Was he waiting for everyone in the neighborhood to go to sleep, waiting for her to be in the depths of slumber before sneaking into the house?

Remembering that she'd seen a pair of binoculars on a shelf in Miranda's bedroom closet, she relocked the door, raced into the bedroom and grabbed them from the shelf.

She returned to the front door and focused them on the driver of the car. A small sigh of surprise escaped her.

Matt.

Her first, gut reaction was anger. What in the hell did he think he was doing sitting out there in the middle of the night?

But the anger flashed quick and hot, then died and instead a lump of emotion rose up in her throat.

He was doing something nobody had ever really done for her in her entire life. He was protecting her, that's what he was doing. Because he cared. She squeezed her eyes closed against a sudden sting of tears and realized if she wasn't careful, she'd care back.

IT WAS SEVEN-THIRTY the next morning when Matt knocked on Jenna's door. He'd spent the endlessly long night in his car keeping an eye on the place, then at six-thirty had raced to his office, showered and changed clothes, and returned.

He didn't want her to know that he'd been on watch duty through the night and hoped his exhaustion didn't show on his face.

When she opened the door her smile energized him. She was dressed in a pair of jeans and a blue t-shirt that stretched across her full breasts and did amazing things to her eyes.

"Good morning," he said. "Ready?"

"Ready," she replied and stepped out of the house. She pulled the door shut, then checked to make sure it had locked. "Did you sleep well?" she asked as they walked to his patrol car.

"Like a log," he lied. "What about you?"

"It took me a while to get to sleep, but once I did, I slept fine," she replied. "What are the plans for today?"

"I thought maybe you could spend the day coordinating in the conference room and I'm going to hit the streets once again to talk to people we might have missed in our preliminary round of interviews."

"So you intend to shove me into the conference room and lock the door. I don't think so, Matt," she exclaimed.

"Then you can come with me to do some interviewing," he said grudgingly.

"That's better." She flashed him one of her cheeky grins and his heart did a little somersault.

It was odd. He'd dated Natalie for four years before he'd finally proposed to her. Theirs had been a relationship that had built slowly, starting with friendship and then blossoming into something deeper and lasting.

He'd known Jenna less than a week and yet she stirred something deep inside him. The need to protect, a desire to make her smile, a yearning to be somebody she knew she could depend on, those things were all there inside of him, along with a primal desire for her.

He'd never felt such a sharp connection so quickly with anyone in his life and he knew when the time came to tell her goodbye it was going to be extremely difficult.

"You're quiet," she said, pulling him from his thoughts.

"Just mulling things over in my head," he replied as he parked in front of the office. It was going to be a long day with no sleep the night before and he definitely needed to assign one of his deputies to sit in front of her house tonight. He did not want that house to be without protection, especially through the dark hours of the night, but he knew if he tried to stay awake all night again he'd crash and burn.

They were met by Joey at the door. "Sheriff, I just got a call from Glen Talbot. He says his wife has been murdered and we need to get over there right away."

"Get Abe and Jerry to meet us there," Matt said and then he and Jenna ran back to his car, Matt silently cursing beneath his breath. He started his car and slammed it into gear, then took off in the direction of the Talbot home on the edge of town.

"The bastard fooled us," Jenna exclaimed. She leaned forward and slammed her palm against the dashboard. "It was supposed to be me. Damn it, he was supposed to come after me." She leaned back and looked at him. "Tell me about the Talbots."

"Glen and Marianne Talbot. He farms and she is a stay-at-home wife. They're in their thirties and Marianne has brown hair. I'm not sure about the color of her eyes." Matt wanted to punch something. Who was this killer? How many more women would wind up dead before the monster was caught?

"If this is our man, then he's broken his pattern," Jenna said, her tone troubled. "This is the first married woman he's gone after. If she got the roses, I wonder how she explained them to her husband?"

"We'll know soon enough," Matt replied as he turned onto the lane that led to the Talbot farmhouse.

The early morning light cast a golden glow on the neat home with its expansive front yard.

The scene would have been peaceful had it not been for the man standing in the middle of the yard, his shirt covered with blood.

"God, I'm tired of this job," Jenna murmured.

As Matt pulled his car to a halt, Glen Talbot staggered forward, releasing deep, wrenching sobs as he approached their vehicle.

"She's dead," he cried as Matt and Jenna got out of the car. The scene was so reminiscent of what they had just gone through at Carolyn Cox's place.

"Oh, God, somebody killed her," Glen screamed. "I shouldn't have left the house. I should have been here." He collapsed to the ground.

At that moment Abe and Jerry pulled up. "Abe, take care of Glen. Jenna and I are going inside."

He glanced at her and saw a look of dread coupled with fierce determination on her face. He opened his trunk and withdrew booties and gloves and then together they approached the front door.

They'd asked no questions of Glen, but Matt assumed that Marianne would be in the bedroom like the other two victims.

He went there first, hoping that maybe Glen was wrong, that there was still breath in Marianne, that somehow they weren't too late to save her.

He didn't even have to walk into the room to know

that, indeed, it was too late for Marianne. She lay in the center of the king-sized bed, a knife protruding from her chest and her eyes frozen open in death.

He closed his eyes, for a moment overwhelmed with guilt. He was the sheriff and he wasn't keeping the women in his town safe.

It was Jenna's hand touching his shoulder that pulled him from that dark place. He gave her a grateful look and then stepped closer to the victim.

"This isn't the work of our man," Jenna said.

He knew exactly what had prompted her words. There was no rose on Marianne's chest. "Maybe he got in a hurry, didn't have time to do it the way he wanted," Matt offered.

Jenna frowned thoughtfully. "I don't think so, but maybe." She moved closer to the bed. "There also don't appear to be any ligature marks around her wrists. That's different from our other victims, too."

"I'll get Abe and Jerry in here to collect whatever they can find and call for the coroner and you and I can talk to Glen and see what he can tell us."

Before they went outside they walked through the house to the kitchen. Dirty dishes were in the sink and a small paper bag set on the counter, but there was no vase holding five roses.

"Maybe she threw them out or hid them from Glen," Matt said more to himself than to Jenna.

"That wouldn't explain why he didn't leave one on her body," she replied.

When they went back outside Glen was seated on the ground as if in a stupor. Matt instructed his deputies and called for the coroner, then approached the man.

"Glen, I know this is tough, but we need to find out what happened here this morning," Matt said.

Glen looked up at Matt, his features twisted. "I know what happened this morning. I left the house and that serial killer got inside and murdered my wife." He buried his face in his hands.

Matt laid a hand on Glen's shoulder. "What time did you leave the house this morning and where did you go?"

The July sun was growing hotter by the minute, but Matt scarcely noticed as he tried to get information from the grieving husband.

Once again Glen raised his head and then wearily got to his feet to face Matt and Jenna. "I got up about two and packed up my fishing gear. It was probably close to three when I left the house and went down to the pond to do some fishing."

"Do you do that often? Get up in the middle of the night to go to the pond?" Jenna asked.

Glen shrugged. "Maybe once or twice a week. I sometimes have trouble sleeping and it always seems senseless just to stay in bed."

He looked back at Matt and once again his

features contorted in a mask of grief. "You've got to catch him, Matt. You have to catch the man who killed my Marianne."

"I'm working on it," he replied. "What time did you come back here to the house?" He needed to keep Glen focused on the facts while everything was still fresh in his mind.

"I was out on the pond until about six and then realized I'd left the lunch I'd packed on the kitchen counter, so I decided to come back and grab my lunch sack. That's when I found her."

"Was your wife awake when you left the house at three?" Jenna asked.

"Nah, Marianne didn't like to get out of bed until near noon," he replied.

And on it went, questions and answers and investigation. Photos were taken, evidence collected and the coroner arrived. The deputies left to interview neighbors, although Matt had little hope that they would be able to add any information. The nearest neighbor to the Talbot farm was nearly a mile down the road.

It was after five when all that could be done had been done. Matt was beyond exhausted, functioning solely on adrenaline and Jenna looked just as weary.

"Food is the first order of business," he said once they were in his car.

"Sounds good to me," she agreed.

"We'll order from the café and they can deliver to

the office. I can write up my reports and go over everything we have so far."

He tightened his grip on the steering wheel. "I feel so damn helpless. Young women are dying and I can't stop it from happening."

"I'm fairly certain that Marianne wasn't killed by our man. I think her husband killed her and tried to take advantage of the fact that there is a killer working in town," Jenna said. "The roses were missing from the scene and that's the one thing you've managed to keep from the general public."

"I keep thinking maybe if she got them she tossed them, knowing they didn't come from Glen," he replied.

"The missing roses aren't the only reason I'd bet on Glen. He didn't cry."

Matt glanced at her in surprise. "He sobbed and wailed," he protested.

"Without tears," she replied. "And when he said that Marianne often slept until noon, there was a faint edge of scorn in his voice. I'll bet you that if you dig into that marriage you'll find it wasn't a happy one and that this is a domestic crime, not the work of our serial killer."

"I'll take that bet," he said after a moment's consideration.

It was just after six when they sat in the conference room to eat the meals that had been delivered by Leroy. Matt had ordered the special of a hot roast beef sandwich and a piece of Michael's lemon meringue pie and Jenna had opted for a burger and fries.

"Talk to me about something other than murders," Jenna said as she plunged her straw up and down in her soda glass.

"Like what? What do you want to talk about?" he asked.

"Anything. What do you do when you aren't sheriffing, what kind of movies do you like, what's your favorite food?"

"I like taking drives in the country and tinkering with a car I've been restoring. I don't watch many movies and my favorite food is whatever is in front of me at the time," he replied. "What about you? What do you do when you aren't FBIing?"

She frowned, the gesture doing nothing to detract from her prettiness. "It seems like I'm working all the time. My friend Sam says that I'm obsessed with work so I don't have to deal with the fact that I have no personal life. He's one to talk, he's just like me."

Matt leaned back in his chair and looked at her thoughtfully. "So why don't you have a personal life? What do you see for yourself in the future? What plans and dreams do you have?"

She shook her head. "I never think about the future. I just live for each day and if I make it to another one, then it's all good. I also don't have any plans or dreams." She broke eye contact with him and picked up another fry. "Even when I was a kid, the only thing important was getting through the day. Now, tell me about your wife."

She broke his heart more than just a little bit. How could there be life without hopes and dreams? He knew she'd changed the subject so that they wouldn't be talking about her.

"Natalie liked to laugh and go for long walks. She believed in helping others and charitable causes. She loved dogs and kids and me."

"You saved a lot of people that day," Jenna said as if to temper the cost of his loss.

"I know. I've thought about it a million times, wondering if I should have done anything different, but realized I did what I thought was best at the time. It took a while, but I've made peace with it. Now tell me something else about Jenna Taylor, something that nobody else knows."

She smiled and for a moment in the warmth of that smile he saw the woman she could be, the woman she was meant to be. "When I was nine I hid a dog in my bedroom for almost a month. It was one of the few times we lived in a rental house where I had my own room. The dog was a stray, a mutt that stank to high heaven, but I didn't care. Every night I let that stinking, slobbering dog into my bed where he cuddled up against me and licked my cheek with his stinky breath."

"What did you call him?" Matt asked, entranced by the sparkle in her eyes as she spoke of the dog.

"Rover, of course. Rover was my best friend, the first thing I think I ever really loved."

"Your mother didn't know he was there?"

She released a dry laugh. "Most of the time my mother didn't know I was there. I'd sneak him in and out before and after school when she was usually passed out and I never heard him make a sound whenever I was in the room with him."

"What happened to him?" Matt asked.

Instantly the warmth in her eyes disappeared, making him sorry he'd asked the question. She stared at the whiteboard behind him and drew a deep sigh.

"I guess I got too confident and thought Rover understood the danger of making noise. This particular morning I left him in my room when I went to school. I made sure he had food and water and put newspapers down for him to do his business. I thought I'd left him everything he needed to be without me for the day, but he must have barked or something. I got home from school and he was gone. My mother's boyfriend at the time told me he'd been taken to the pound and they were going to put him to sleep."

His heart ached for the little girl who'd had nothing to love but a stray dog who would be taken away from her. "I'm sorry, Jenna. I'm so damn sorry that you had to live your childhood. I wish you could have had mine."

She looked back at him and there was a softness in her eyes. "You're a nice man, Matt. It's been a true pleasure getting to know you. Now let's finish eating and see what order we can make of this mess." She'd effectively closed the door on sharing anything else personal.

For the next four hours they sat and worked on the murder file for their newest victim. Throughout those hours Matt's deputies checked in with what information they had gleaned by speaking with friends and family members.

It was just after ten when Matt scooted back from the table, too exhausted to do anything further. "I've got to call it a night."

"Me, too," Jenna agreed.

They didn't speak as they got into the car and drove to Miranda's place. Matt was just too exhausted to attempt to make small talk.

He'd made arrangements for Tom Willard, one of his deputies who worked the night shift, to sit in front of Miranda's house for the night. At least he would sleep well knowing she was protected.

He pulled up in front of the house with a weary sigh. "I want to check it out before I leave you here alone," he said as they got out of the car.

He stood just behind her as she unlocked the door, able to smell the faint scent of her lingering perfume in the hot, humid air.

"How about you check the kitchen and living room

and I'll check the bedrooms," she said as they stepped into the foyer. She pulled her gun as he drew his.

They parted ways and Matt headed for the kitchen while she disappeared down the hallway. There was no indication that any of the windows or doors had been messed with, nothing to make him worry that somebody had gotten into the house.

He checked the pantry and any place else big enough for a grown man to hide. "I'm clear, Jenna. What about you?" he yelled down the hallway.

There was no reply.

"Jenna?" he called again.

When there was still no answer his heart banged hard against his ribs. With his gun gripped firmly in both hands, he made his way down the hallway.

He checked the bathroom as he passed, then sighed in relief as he saw her standing just inside the guest room. "Jenna, why didn't you answer me?" he asked as his heart slowed to a more normal pace.

As he stepped into the room he realized what had made her freeze in her tracks. In the center of the bed was a single long-stem red rose.

Even though he knew it was coming, the sight of it in this house they'd believed was secured, on the bed where she slept, shocked him. "Jenna," he said as he turned to look at her.

Before he could continue, she nodded. "I'll pack my bags."

He breathed a sigh of relief. He had no idea what had made her change her mind. Yesterday she'd been adamant that she would stay here until the killer came with the final rose.

As she pulled her suitcase from the closet he noticed that her hands trembled and a new surge of protectiveness welled up inside him. The FBI agent with the fierce attitude was definitely afraid.

Chapter Nine

Jenna was afraid. As she packed her bags to leave this house she was shocked by the edge of fear that whispered through her.

Why now? She couldn't remember the last time she'd felt fear. Certainly she'd faced danger before. As recently as yesterday when the first rose arrived, she hadn't felt any real fear.

But things were different now and she didn't know why. She only knew she wanted away from here. She wanted the safety of Matt's house, the safety of his presence nearby.

Matt made the call to get a couple of deputies over to collect any evidence that the killer might have left behind, but Jenna wasn't optimistic that he'd made a mistake. He'd been so careful so far.

As Matt drove her to his house, she closed her eyes and fought against the strange emotions that coursed through her.

Maybe it was the memories of Rover that had made her feel so oddly vulnerable. Or maybe it had been the softness in Matt's eyes when she'd shared that story with him.

She wanted to believe that it was nothing more than the sight of that rose in a house she thought was secure. She opened her eyes and gazed at Matt in the light from the dashboard.

"He has to have a key to Miranda's house. The doors and windows weren't broken or jimmied. The only way he could have gotten in there was having a key to the front or backdoor," she said.

Matt frowned. He looked exhausted and she knew he probably hadn't slept the night before which meant he had to be ready to fall over. "The only person I know who had a key to her place is Maggie Wendt."

"Then we need to talk to her again and find out if she gave a copy of the key to anyone else or if she knew if Miranda gave somebody else the key."

"I'll check with her first thing in the morning. I'm meeting with the mayor at ten. He wants an update and to be able to give the women of this town some sort of assurance that we're on top of this."

"At the moment all I want to be on top of is a nice soft bed," she replied drily.

"Why don't you sit tight tomorrow at my place?" he said. "Nobody will know you're there. You've been pushing yourself pretty hard and maybe a day off will be good for you."

She shot him a sharp glance, wondering if he sensed how off-kilter she felt? Her first instinct was to give him a resounding no thanks, but the idea of staying inside, maybe cooking a decent meal and watching television was surprisingly appealing.

"Maybe I will do that," she said, although she suspected by morning she'd be chomping at the bit, ready to get out and find the bastard who was terrorizing town.

"Wow, you're so close to the office," she exclaimed as he pulled into the driveway of an attractive two-story home just off Main Street.

"I keep my official car parked in front of the office and usually walk to work," he replied as he shut off the engine.

"Nobody followed us?" she asked. She hadn't missed the way he'd checked his rearview mirror on the drive from Miranda's.

"Not a soul. I'll get your suitcase." As they got out of the car Jenna grabbed the small overnight bag and Matt lifted the bigger suitcase from the backseat.

As he unlocked the door she realized she was intrigued to see the space where he lived. As a profiler she knew you could often tell a lot about a person by viewing the choices they made in their personal space.

They walked into a foyer with gleaming wooden

floors and a standing oak coatrack that held nothing at the moment.

The living room looked lived in but not cluttered. A newspaper was open on the coffee table and a mug sat next to it. The sofa was navy blue and held throw pillows in red and navy. A recliner faced the wall shelving unit that held the television, a stereo system and pictures of two dark-haired women she assumed were his sisters.

It felt like what she'd always believed a home should be like, warm and inviting. "Nice," she said as she set her overnight bag on the plush beige carpeting.

He set down the suitcase. "Let me show you the rest of the place," he said.

She followed him into a bright, airy kitchen with white cabinets and accents of red. A basket of fruit decorated the center of the round oak table.

"This doesn't have the flavor of a bachelor pad," she said.

He smiled. "I never intended it to be a bachelor pad. It was always meant to be a home for a family."

"How long have you lived here?" she asked as they left the kitchen and returned to the living room.

"Two years. Before that I was renting a place on the north side of town. But two years ago was about the time my grief over Natalie started to ease and I started looking forward again."

She eyed him curiously. "But it must be difficult, to think about doing it all over with somebody else?"

"Not at all. Do I wish Natalie hadn't died? Of course, but one of the things I learned with her was how good love feels, how important it is in my life and I want that again, that magic of loving somebody and knowing I'm loved back."

Once again she had the feeling that this man could be dangerous to her, that he could make her wish for things she'd never wished for before, that he could make her believe things that had always felt impossible.

"I'm really beat, could you show me to my room?" she asked, suddenly eager to escape his presence.

She followed him up the stairs where he led her to a pleasant room decorated in cool shades of blue. The bed was a double and the pillows looked big and fluffy and a sudden exhaustion overwhelmed her.

"The bathroom is across the hall and my room is at the end if you need anything," Matt said as he placed her suitcase on the bed.

"Thanks, I'll be fine." She breathed a sigh of relief as he left the room. It had probably been a mistake coming here, but even though she'd expected to find another rose, she hadn't expected her reaction.

She didn't want to think about it anymore. She didn't want to think about anything. She just wanted the sweet oblivion of sleep.

It took her only minutes to get into her silk night-gown and pad across the hall to the bathroom. She washed her face and brushed her teeth, avoiding her own reflection in the mirror.

She was afraid of what she might see in her own eyes, a softness for the man who had taken her in, a desire for him and all the things he wanted in his life.

She wasn't the woman for him. She had no hopes and dreams. When they found this killer she'd go back to her real life in an apartment that had never felt like home, navigating through life as she always had—alone.

She thought sleep would be difficult but the moment she got into bed and closed her eyes, she slept. When she next opened her eyes she could hear the sound of birds singing outside the window and the sun was already climbing up the eastern sky.

She sat up and looked at the clock next to the bed. She gasped in surprise. After eight! She couldn't remember the last time she'd slept so late.

By the time she'd taken a quick shower and dressed, she sensed that she was alone in the house even though she smelled the scent of coffee. Matt would have left for the office by now and she tried to work up some irritation that he hadn't awakened her to go in with him, but the truth was she was glad she hadn't.

The past week had been a rush of crazy emotions, of long hours and intensity. She needed to step back from everything and take a moment to breathe and that's exactly what she intended to do.

She was confident that Matt and his team would continue to do everything within their means without her. For a small-town force, they were definitely on the ball. She'd found each and every one of his detectives smart and highly motivated to catch the killer.

In the kitchen she found not only a pot of coffee ready to be consumed, but also a brief note from Matt telling her that he hoped she had a good day and that if nothing unexpected happened, he'd try to be back at the house by around five or six.

She poured herself a cup of coffee and carried it with her as she walked through the living room to the window by the front door where she peered outside and saw a patrol car parked at the curb with Joey seated behind the wheel.

With a small shake of her head she left the window and returned to the kitchen where she sat at the table. Matt was determined to provide a certain level of protection for her whether she wanted it or not.

He'd accused her of being stubborn, but she had a feeling he wasn't exactly a slacker in that particular department, either.

A surge of warmth filled her as she continued to think about Matt. He would make some woman a wonderful husband. Not only was he hot as hell, he was also a good man with a great sense of humor and a sharp intelligence that could challenge any woman.

"But not for me," she murmured aloud. Marriage

and kids and happily-ever-after had never been on her list of things to do before she died.

As if to confirm who she was and where she belonged, she picked up her cell phone and called Sam. He answered on the second ring.

"Where are you?" she asked.

"In a tiny motel room in Mayville, Kansas," he replied.

"What are you working on?"

"I was sent out here yesterday to check out a hate crime. A gay man was beaten to death by another man, but I think it's more about a drug deal gone wrong than any hatred. I'll probably head back to the field office sometime in the morning. When are you coming back?"

She knew the smart thing to do would be to head back to Kansas City before the killer caught a lucky break and caught her off guard. She should get out of town so that Matt didn't feel the responsibility of keeping her safe. More importantly she should leave before her heart got any more involved with him than it already was.

"I don't know," she said, finally answering Sam's question. "I'd like to see this thing through to the end," she said, unsure if she was referring to catching the killer or seeing where her feelings for Matt might take her. "But I'm thinking maybe I'll head back in the next week or so."

They chatted about the case for a few minutes and she caught him up on everything that had happened since she'd arrived in town.

When they finally hung up Jenna poured herself another cup of coffee and returned to her seat at the table.

She was the first one to admit that she'd always been a little reckless, fearless when it came to the possibility of death.

But that's exactly what she felt now…fear and an intense desire to stay alive. She had a feeling it had to do with Matt and that scared the hell out of her.

IT HAD BEEN YET another day of sheer frustration. As Matt walked the few blocks from the office to his house, he tried to shrug off the foul mood that had been growing with every dead end he and his deputies had met throughout the day.

At least he hadn't had the worry of wondering if Jenna was in trouble. He didn't think anyone knew she was in his house except the deputies he'd told. If the killer couldn't find her, then he couldn't do her any harm.

Matt had spoken to her twice during the day and it had comforted him to know she was in his house with Joey playing watchdog outside.

As Joey's car came into sight he raised a hand in greeting. The young deputy got out of the car and greeted him with a smile. "Nothing to report, sir. It's been real quiet all day."

Matt clapped him on the shoulder. "And boring. I know this gig wasn't exactly how you wanted to spend your day, but I appreciate your work to help keep Agent Taylor safe."

Joey nodded. "Sometimes it's not all about blazing guns and danger. It's just about keeping somebody safe."

Matt nodded. "There's one other thing I want you to do for me before you go off duty. I'd like you to swing by Miranda's house and see if there's a rose anywhere in the house or outside."

Joey frowned. "That would be number three, right?"

Tension twisted in Matt's stomach. "Yeah, and if our killer stays on track, that means we're halfway to the next murder victim and it's going to be Jenna."

"But we aren't going to let that happen, are we?" Joey said with fierce determination.

"Not while there's breath in my body," Matt replied. "Call me after you check Miranda's, and thanks, Joey, for always doing a great job."

As Matt headed to the front door Joey got into his patrol car and pulled away from the curb. Joey was like a young pup, eager to please and responded well to praise. Someday he was going to be a terrific lawman; all he needed was a little more maturity and experience.

All thoughts of Joey fled his mind as he stepped through the front door and was greeted with the scent of pungent tomato sauce and spicy garlic.

Jenna must have heard the door open for she stepped from the kitchen into the living room with her gun in hand. "Hi, honey, I'm home," he said. "And you know it always turns me on when you greet me with a gun."

"Don't tempt me to pull the trigger," she replied as she lowered the gun.

She looked well rested and amazingly gorgeous in a turquoise summer shift that exposed the length of her shapely legs and electrified the blue of her eyes.

"I smell something good," he said as he followed her into the kitchen.

"I hope you like spaghetti and meatballs." She moved to stand by the stove and picked up a wooden spoon to stir the sauce.

She looked right in his kitchen. He knew it was a chauvinistic thought, but he couldn't help it. She looked like she belonged here and in the depths of his heart, no matter how crazy it seemed, no matter how short the time had been since they'd met, he realized he wanted her to belong here.

It was an ache inside of him, the desire to love her as she'd never been loved before, to provide a place in his arms where she would always feel safe, would always feel cherished.

"Matt? Spaghetti and meatballs? Love it or hate it?"

She looked at him expectantly and he realized he hadn't answered her. "Love it," he said.

"It's going to be ready in about fifteen minutes. Why don't you go change your clothes and wash up or whatever you do and by then I'll have it on the table."

"Sounds like a plan," he agreed. He left the kitchen and went upstairs to his bedroom where he changed from his uniform into a pair of comfortable jeans and a white T-shirt.

When he got back to the kitchen she had placed salad and bread on the table and was in the process of adding a big bowl of spaghetti with fist-sized meatballs.

"Wow, I didn't realize you could cook," he said.

She gestured him into a chair and flashed him one of her charming smiles. "I can cook. I'm just not sure if I'm a good cook. I don't have time to do it much." She joined him at the table. "So tell me about your day."

He shook his head. "Nope. The rule around here is that you don't shoptalk while you eat."

"Then I doubt if we'll have anything to say," she replied.

He grinned at her. "Oh, Jenna, you underestimate my ability to talk about nothing and your own ability to be a fascinating conversationalist."

She laughed and shook her head. "If I didn't know any better I'd bet you were trying to charm me right into your bed."

He picked up his fork and quirked his eyebrow upward. "What makes you think I'm not?"

Her cheeks turned pink as she handed him the bread. "Because you know it wouldn't be a good idea," she replied. "Matt, I'm a temporary woman and you're a forever kind of guy. Oil and water, Matt, and pretending we're anything different would be foolish."

"Who says you can't be foolish once in a while?" he replied.

"Okay, I'm making a new rule," she exclaimed. "No shoptalk and no talking about sex during dinner."

He smiled. "Okay, I accept your new rule, but that doesn't mean I can't think about sex." She shot him a dirty look, but there was definitely a wicked little sparkle in her eyes.

Dinner conversation was light and pleasant. Matt shared with her stories about the small town of Bridgewater and about life with his parents and sisters. Jenna seemed curious about his family life and he wanted to satisfy her curiosity.

She seemed most interested in the everyday normalcy of his family life. He told her about pancakes on Sunday mornings and Friday night charades and when he talked about those long-ago days he was reminded again of how lucky he'd been to have had loving parents who had taught him how to love and be loved.

It was after the meal was finished, the dishes were done and the two were settled back at the table with coffee that the talk turned to business.

"Still no progress on where the roses might have

come from," he said, aware of the frustration that laced his tone. "Lab reports came back today on Miranda. There were no drugs or alcohol in her system."

"I didn't expect there to be," she replied. "Miranda was a health nut and she was adamantly against drugs. The only way she would have had anything in her system would be if the killer had forced her to take something." She curled her fingers around her cup. "I'm guessing nobody saw anything when that rose was left at Miranda's yesterday?"

"We canvassed the area and spoke to all the neighbors. Nobody saw anything."

She frowned. "We aren't chasing a ghost. Somebody has to have seen something at one of these scenes."

"We haven't found them yet."

"Instead of putting a guard on me, you should have a man on our two top suspects, Dr. Johnson and Leroy."

"What about Bud? He has been on the top of our list."

She leaned back in the chair. "I've been doing a lot of thinking about all this today and I don't think Bud is our man. You could arrest him for being an arrogant ass, but I think that's probably all he's guilty of."

Matt smiled. "If I started arresting all the men guilty of that, my jail wouldn't be able to hold them all. One thing that will make your day—according to Marianne's friends, she was getting ready to kick Glen to the curb. The farm and pretty much everything they owned was in Marianne's name. It seems she bought the place before they got married with inheritance money she'd received."

"So if there had been a divorce Glen would have walked away with nothing. Sounds like a motive for murder to me," she replied.

He nodded. "We'll work at getting our ducks in a row and I'm figuring we can make an arrest in that case within a week or so."

"But that gets us no closer to solving Miranda's and Carolyn's murders."

"Nor does it get us any closer to who has left you two roses." He took a sip of his coffee, needing the warmth to ease the chill that swept through him as he thought of somebody harming her. "I don't suppose you've considered leaving town?" Although he wasn't ready to tell her goodbye, if that's what it took to keep her safe, then he'd help her pack her bags.

She leaned forward, bringing with her that evocative scent that stirred a primal lust inside him. "To be honest, I've spent the day considering all my options and leaving town was definitely one I considered, then dismissed."

"Why not leave? Why not assure your own safety?"

He watched the play of emotions that raced across her features. There was a whisper of fear, a hint of sheer stubbornness and something else, something that gave Matt hope.

"Two things made me decide to stay. I hope that as long as I'm the target, then he isn't targeting any other woman," she said.

"You said one of the things. What's the other?" he asked. His breath caught in his chest as he realized he wanted her answer to be him.

"I'm not a quitter," she replied. "I don't give up when things get tough. I want to see this thing through to the end."

At that moment Matt's cell phone rang. He plucked it from his pocket and answered to hear Joey's voice. "Sheriff, it's here, a rose at Miranda's. It was on the front porch when I got here. I bagged it and tagged it."

"Thanks, Joey." Even though Matt had been expecting it, his heart beat a heightened rhythm of anxiety as he clicked off and looked at Jenna.

"What's up?" she asked.

"Joey checked out Miranda's place for me and he found another rose." He watched as her eyes deepened in hue. "That makes three, Jenna. If our killer maintains his routine, then within three days, this will be over."

Neither of them spoke the words that he knew they were both thinking, that in three days' time either the killer would be caught or Jenna would be killed.

Chapter Ten

"Maggie Wendt insists she never gave the key to Miranda's house to anyone and she has no idea who Miranda might have given a copy to," Matt said.

Darkness had fallen outside and he'd just returned from Miranda's where he'd met Joey.

"Leroy might have had access to her keys at the café," Jenna replied, as she thought about the young waitress who had found Miranda's body.

"It's possible any number of people might have been able to get to them at the café. I'll need to find out where the waitresses store their purses and other personal things when they're working." He leaned back in his chair and swept his fingers through his thick dark hair.

For a moment his eyes held hers, and in their depths she was a simmering fire that had nothing to do with the facts of the case.

Jenna's fingers hummed with the memory of how

his hair had felt, so rich and silky when she'd tangled her fingers in it when they'd made love.

It was almost ten o'clock and for the last several hours they had chewed over the case, thrown around ideas and argued theories, and through it all there had been a simmering tension between them.

Jenna knew it was desire, a desire built on the realization that her time here with him was quickly coming to an end.

She'd told him she wanted to see this through to its conclusion, but in reality she had a job to get back to and she couldn't remain in the town of Bridgewater, Texas, forever.

She hoped that the killer would come after her and she'd manage to get him under arrest. If she survived an attack and for some reason the killer got away, she believed it would still be time for her to leave Bridgewater.

Eventually Matt and his men would get the guilty and if Matt decided he wanted official FBI involvement, then he could send in a request and agents would be dispatched to help him with the investigation.

In any case, she felt it in her heart, in her soul, that it was time to leave and get back to her real life and leave this charming little Texas town behind.

"I'm calling it a night," she said as she got up from the table. "I can't think about all this another minute. My brain is completely fried."

"I feel the same way," he agreed. He got up and carried their cups to the sink and then shut off the coffeepot.

Moments later as she climbed the stairs to the guest bedroom she was acutely conscious of Matt just behind her. One more time, she thought as she reached her bedroom door. Was it so wrong of her to want one more time in his arms, to desire the feel of his heartbeat next to hers? She might be dead in three days. Why not steal one last moment of pleasure with him.

She turned to face him. "If you're fairly certain that Glen Talbot killed his wife, then doesn't that mean I won our little bet?"

His gray eyes flared with a hot shine that nearly scorched her. "I think you're right," he said and moved a step closer to her. "So I guess I have to pay up. I wouldn't want to renege on a bet. Although we didn't say specifically what the bet was for, I think a kiss would be appropriate."

Her knees weakened as he took another step toward her, so close that her breasts touched his chest and she fought against a shiver of pleasure that threatened to sweep up her spine.

"You know if I kiss you I'll want more," he said, his voice low and husky.

"I know if you kiss me, I'll want more," she replied and raced her tongue over her upper lip in anticipation of what was to come.

She didn't know for sure if it was the words she'd

spoken or the slide of her tongue, but one or both seemed to enflame him, for he grabbed her to him and crashed his mouth to hers.

The kiss was hot and hungry and just that quickly Jenna felt her bones melting as hunger for him flamed inside her.

She wrapped her arms around his neck and molded her body to his and as always when she was in his arms she felt safe and right.

When the kiss ended she took a step into her bedroom, but he caught her by the arm and shook his head. "No, I want you in my room. I want you in my bed."

He didn't give her a chance to reply, but instead scooped her up in his arms and carried her down the hallway toward the master bedroom.

She'd been in there earlier in the day, wanting to see his personal space. She'd never tell him that she'd hugged his pillow, smelling the scent of him and that it had calmed her nerves.

Now the last thing she felt as he laid her on the bed was calm. Every muscle in her body ached for him, every nerve ending sang with the anticipation of the pleasure she knew was about to come.

He stood by the side of the bed and ripped his T-shirt over his head and then as he took off his jeans, she sat up and pulled her sundress over her head.

The only illumination was a stream of moonlight playing through the thin, gauzy curtains at the bank of windows. He was stunning in the moonlight, a study of sinewy muscle and want.

Her heart beat frantically as he joined her on the bed and their lips met once again in a kiss that stole all rational thought from her mind.

It was impossible to think as he removed her bra and gently cupped her breasts and his mouth kissed down the length of her neck. It was impossible to think when his hands swept down her stomach and slowly pulled off her panties.

The last time they had made love it had been frantic and fast with little time for foreplay, but this time it was slow and easy, as if they had the rest of their lives to complete what they had started.

She discovered all the places on his body that made him groan with pleasure when she touched him. In turn he found those sensitive spots on her that electrified her.

No matter how she tried to keep her mind disengaged and focus solely on the physical pleasure of making love to Matt, she couldn't stop the mental connection with him from happening.

He seemed intent to hold her gaze as he caressed her, as if making love to her mind as well as her body. Even when she closed her eyes she could feel him not just against her body, but touching her places inside where she'd never been touched before.

Matt was a silent lover, saying little with his lips but speaking volumes through his caresses and kisses. He made her feel beautiful. He made her feel special and that was as seductive as anything he could have done.

He brought her to climax and while she was still shuddering in the throes, he entered her. She wrapped her legs around his back, pulling him deeper inside her as wave after wave of pleasure overwhelmed her.

He whispered her name and then began to move against her, stroking in and out in agonizingly slow, exquisitely exhilarating movements that had her once again climbing to a peak.

Sex had never been this way for her, so intense, so personal and she knew it wasn't the act itself but rather the man she shared it with that made the difference.

When she reached her peak again she felt as if she had shattered, and as he stiffened against her and hoarsely cried her name, she captured the moment in her memory to keep forever.

Afterward, when they were both spent and their breathing had returned to a more normal pace she started to get up, but he held her tight.

"Why do you have to run off?" he asked. "Stay here with me. Sleep with me."

She rolled a few inches away from him and propped herself up on one elbow. "I never sleep with a man."

"Why not?" He propped himself up on his elbow to face her.

"I don't know. I guess I've never been with a man I wanted to wake up to in the morning," she replied.

"If you think I'm charming late at night, you should see me first thing in the morning," he exclaimed.

She smiled. First the man had charmed her right out of her dress and now he was seducing her to break all her own rules and spend the night in his bed.

"Come on, Jenna," he whispered. He reached out and stroked a thumb down her cheek. "What are you afraid of? That we might cuddle in the darkness? That you might feel safe and warm?"

"I'm not used to feeling that way," she replied after a moment of silence.

He pulled her against him, her face in the warmth of his chest. "Maybe it's time you get used to it. Just let yourself go, Jenna. Don't think, just relax."

His hand stroked softly down the length of her back and to her surprise she found herself relaxing, melding into the mattress, into him.

Don't think. Listen to what he said, she told herself and closed her eyes. It felt good, to be cradled in his arms with his body heat warming her.

A sweet drowsiness swept over her and she'd nearly fallen asleep when she felt his breath close to her ear.

"You know, I could be in love with you if you'd let me," he murmured.

She stiffened and raised her head to look at him. "Oh, Matt, don't. Don't fall in love with a woman like me. Don't you remember, I have no hopes or dreams for the future?"

He pulled her close and once again stroked down the length of her back. "Don't worry about it, I have enough hopes and dreams for the both of us."

He fell asleep almost immediately, but she remained awake, a terrible dread filling her. She was going to break his heart and it didn't make her feel any better that she'd warned him ahead of time.

What was worse, she had a feeling that his wasn't the only heart that might be broken when this was all said and done.

MATT WOKE UP at dawn and she was gone, the part of the bed where she had been cold to his touch. There had been several times in the night when he'd reached out and been comforted by her warm body close to his. Still, he wasn't surprised that with the dawn she was gone, as if she'd only been a wonderful dream.

He remained in bed thinking about Jenna and his feelings for her. He'd probably scared her off by baring his heart the night before.

And yet he knew she had a depth of feelings for him, too. She might try to deny it, but he felt it emanating from her whenever they were together; he saw it in her eyes when she thought he wasn't looking.

They were good together, both as partners and as lovers, and he wanted more. He wanted a lifetime with her. Whether she knew it or not, she needed him. She needed him to give her dreams, to give her laughter, but more importantly he'd never met a woman who so desperately needed to be loved. And he was just the man to do it.

All he had to do was convince her.

He smelled coffee, letting him know she'd been up for a while. He got out of bed and padded into the bathroom for a quick shower.

Twenty minutes later he entered the kitchen to find her dressed for the day and seated at the table. "Good morning," he said.

"Morning," she replied.

Instantly he felt the distance wafting from her, an invisible wall that kept her from looking at him in the eyes, warning him not to tread too close.

"Did you sleep well?" He walked to the counter and poured himself a cup of coffee.

"Not really." She finally looked at him with cool blue eyes. "I have no intention of hanging out here all day. I'm going to walk around a little on Main Street, talk to some of the people and see if I can learn any more information than what we already have."

"Do you really think that's a good idea?" He sat at the table opposite her.

She shrugged. "I don't necessarily think it's a bad idea. There are still three roses to go. I'm betting our killer won't jump the gun and that he'll stick to his ritual and need to deliver them all over the next three days."

"And what if you're wrong?" he asked.

"Then I guess I'll lose the bet." She turned her gaze out the window.

Matt studied her profile, loving the way the sun caressed her features, discouraged by the stubborn thrust of her chin. He knew that it was futile to try to argue with her. She would do what she decided, not what he wanted her to do.

Love for her swelled in his chest. She was what he wanted in his life and he knew that he was what she needed in hers.

"You know, there's an FBI field office in Dallas," he finally said. "It wouldn't be such a bad commute from here."

She shot her gaze to him. "Why would you tell me that?"

Matt drew a deep breath and decided to speak from his heart. "You know that I'm falling in love with you and I think that if you look deep in your heart, you'll know that you're falling for me, too."

"That's crazy," she replied quickly. "We've known each other for only a week."

"It's not the amount of time that matters, it's the depth of the emotion. I know what it feels like to be in love and I know what's in my heart for you. Jenna, open your heart and I think you'll be surprised to find what's inside."

She scooted back from the table and jumped up as if on fire. She strode to the counter and stood with her back against it, a deep frown on her face. "I warned you, Matt. I told you that I'm not the kind of woman you need in your life. There was only one time in my entire life I hoped for something and I hoped for it with all my heart and all my soul, and that was for my mother to relinquish her rights to me and let me be a part of a real family."

"But whether your mother gave up her rights or not, you were part of the Harris family," he replied as he got to his feet.

She shook her head. "It wasn't the same. To the outside world I was their foster kid, not their daughter. I needed it to be made legal. I needed to know that nobody could come back in and take me away. The Harrises tried for four years with my mother and every time they told me they were going to ask her again, my hope built that maybe this time my mother would love me enough to let me go. Finally I stopped hoping."

Although her words were said calmly and without emotion, Matt saw the tremble in her lower lip, the edge of pain that laced her eyes.

The wound inside her was deep and had festered for a long time and Matt wanted to rip it open in an effort to allow it to heal, but before he could say anything she continued.

"I don't let people get close to me, Matt. I decided a long time ago that I'd never let anyone be important in my life. Miranda sneaked in beneath my defenses, but I won't allow that to happen again. It's how I live. It's how I survive. I have my work and that's all I need."

He stepped closer to her and her eyes flared slightly at his nearness. "Okay, you had a crappy childhood and your mother was a selfish jerk who couldn't or wouldn't give you what you needed. Lots of people have terrible childhoods, but that doesn't mean they close themselves off from life…from love."

He raised a hand and swept a strand of her soft hair from her shoulder and then stroked his thumb down the side of her face. "Jenna, you have a great capacity to love inside you. I know you do, all you have to do is let it out."

She scooted away from him, away from his touch and her features were a cold mask. "I've already made up my mind that I'm leaving here in a week, whether you catch the killer or not by that time. I have a life to get back to."

"That's not a life, that's just an existence," he replied tersely. He wanted to take her by the shoulders and shake her, he wanted to scoop her back up in his arms, run with her to the bedroom and make love to her until her heart opened to him.

"Jenna, I know you care about me," he continued. "And I just wish you'd give me a chance, give us a chance."

"I'm sorry, Matt." Once again she looked away from him, as if unable to hold his gaze. "It just wouldn't work."

"Then she wins again," he said softly. She stiffened and her eyes blazed with a hint of anger as she glared at him. Good, he thought. This was better than the cool, emotionless shell she'd crawled into. "She kept you from having the family you wanted when you were young and her influence now keeps you from reaching out for the future you want. She wins, Jenna, and you lose."

He walked back over to the table and picked up his coffee cup. "You told me you weren't a quitter, but you're quitting on yourself. You're quitting on us." He raised the cup to his lips and drained the last of his coffee and then set the cup back on the table. "Now, you ready to leave? I need to get to work."

He was hoping for an explosion from her. He was hoping he'd be able to pierce through the thick body armor that she wore to keep her heart and her soul safe from harm.

Her nostrils flared and for a moment he thought he was going to get his wish, but she merely drew a deep breath and shoved off from the counter.

"Fine, let's get out of here," she said and headed for the front door.

HE SAT IN HIS CAR UP the street and watched as Matt and Jenna headed down the sidewalk. He'd suspected she might be here, that she'd run to the sheriff when she'd gotten the roses at Miranda's place.

The early morning sunshine played in her hair and he remembered another woman's hair spilling through his fingertips as her blue eyes smiled at him.

The familiar rage built up inside him. Jenna Taylor was just like the others, playing with a man's emotions with no intention of giving away her heart.

He squeezed his hands into fists as his heartbeat accelerated. The thought of piercing her false, betraying heart with his knife made him feel more alive than he'd felt in years.

One thing was certain. He knew Agent Jenna Taylor thought she understood what he was about, how he worked. What she didn't know was that he had no intention of playing his ritual out to the end.

Before the night was over, Jenna Taylor would not only receive two more roses, but the final one that would mark the end of her life.

Chapter Eleven

Jenna wanted to hate him. As she lowered herself on a bench just outside the sheriff's office, she tried to work up a healthy dose of hatred for Matt Buchannan, but she couldn't.

She'd sat inside his office for only a few minutes and already the beginning of a tension headache was starting to knock at the back of her skull.

She'd needed some fresh air and some distance from the man who tantalized her with the offer of all the things she'd told herself she never wanted, she refused to need.

With her gun inside her purse and her purse right next to her side, she felt no fear as she narrowed her eyes against the bright sunshine and leaned back against the bench.

Her mind suddenly filled with a vision of laughing children who looked like Matt and family meals around his kitchen table. She thought of all the stories he'd told her about his childhood, about movie nights with his family and baseball games with his parents and sisters sitting on the bleachers watching him pitch.

The yearning that filled her pierced her with a bittersweet pang. Family. Children. She knew she'd be a good mother because she'd work to be the kind she'd never had.

He'd told her all she had to do was open herself up, allow the love into her heart, but he had no idea how thick was the shield she'd erected around herself from the time she'd been a child.

Emma and George Harris had insisted she go to counseling right after they'd brought her into their home. Once a week for two years she'd gone to talk to a counselor about her life, her mother and what her future might hold.

Intellectually, Jenna had long ago processed the fact that her mother had been a drug addict who'd chosen her lifestyle over her daughter. Jenna had understood that it hadn't been something wrong with her, but rather with the woman who had given birth to her.

But even knowing all that and talking about it ad nauseum hadn't been able to heal the hurt that lingered in her soul, that built the walls of protection that would never allow her to be hurt like that again.

The thought of dropping those barriers terrified her, but the thought of missing out forever on all the things life with Matt had to offer also broke her heart.

She told herself that it was ridiculous to think about

loving Matt. She'd known him for only a week and yet she knew him better, felt more deeply for him than she ever had another man.

The truth was she'd never been more confused in her life. Maybe the best thing to do, the easiest would be to pack her suitcase and move into the motel until she decided to leave town.

She couldn't stand the idea of going back to Matt's house, of seeing the want, the love in his eyes and maintaining her distance.

How she wished Miranda were still alive. How she would love a sit-down, woman-to-woman talk about Matt, about love, about life.

"Catching a little sun, Agent Taylor?"

The familiar deep voice snapped her eyes open and she grabbed her purse to her side as she looked up at Patrick Johnson. "Just relaxing a bit," she replied as every muscle in her body tensed.

"How much longer are you in town?"

"Looking to get rid of me, Dr. Johnson?" she asked.

"Not at all." He offered her a smile that held no warmth. "Whether you stay here or not has nothing to do with me. I just would prefer it if you'd stay out of my personal life, stop talking to people about me."

She sat up straighter on the bench. "We're conducting a murder investigation, Dr. Johnson, and that means we're asking questions and digging into the personal lives of lots of people."

"You aren't even officially on the case," he scoffed.

His overt antipathy toward her vaguely surprised her. Was he threatened by her? Afraid that she might discover something he didn't want her to know?

"Sheriff Buchannan is using me as a consultant," she replied. And I'm using myself as bait, she added mentally.

"Well, if you're spending a lot of time checking me out, then you're wasting your time," he said. "Believe it or not, I have a fairly good reputation in this town and I don't want it tarnished just because I did a little flirting with a pretty new waitress."

At that moment Matt stepped out of the office. "Morning, Patrick," he said. His easy tone didn't quite hide an edge in his voice. "Problems?" He looked from Patrick to Jenna.

"Not at all," Jenna replied quickly. "Patrick and I were just visiting."

"And now I've got to get to work," Patrick said with a glance at his watch. "Nice talking to you," he said to Jenna and then with a nod to Matt, he walked on down the sidewalk toward his office.

"What was that about?" Matt asked.

"I have a feeling he found out that I'd contacted his old girlfriend and he wasn't particularly happy about it," she replied. "But there was no need for you to run out like a knight in shining armor," she said.

He gave her one of the smiles that always warmed

her, that always twisted her heart. "I could be your permanent port in the storm, your knight in shining armor if you'd just let me."

She got up from the bench. "I'm not a princess and I certainly don't need a knight. I can take care of myself. I've been doing it since I was three. I'm going for a walk." She grabbed her purse and started down the sidewalk, conscious of his gaze lingering on her until she reached the next block.

As she came to the shop that sold stained glass, the same place where June Alexander had worked, her breath caught in her chest as she eyed the beautiful creations that hung in the window and caught the morning light.

She stepped inside and a bell tinkled overhead to announce her entry. A thin, older man looked up and greeted her with a smile. "Welcome," he said. "I'm Stan, the owner of this place. If I can help you with anything, just let me know."

For a few minutes Jenna walked around the store, enjoying the variety and beauty of the items for sale. "I understand June Alexander used to work for you," she finally said.

Stan looked at her in surprise. "Yes, she did. Are you a friend of hers?"

Jenna introduced herself and Stan frowned. "Terrible thing what happened to those women. You expect things like that in a big city but not in a small town like Bridgewater. Why did you ask about June?"

"I understand she was dating Patrick Johnson at one time."

Stan narrowed his eyes. "You think Doc Johnson had something to do with what happened to those women?"

"We're just doing some follow-up questioning," she replied.

They chatted for a few more minutes, but Jenna learned nothing more than she'd already known. When she left the store she looked up and down the street, trying to decide where to go next. She didn't want to go back to the sheriff's office with Matt.

The streets were busy with people walking up and down the sidewalks, taking care of errands before the sun got too hot.

She finally settled once again on a bench across the street from the café. Bud. Leroy. Patrick. The three names of their top suspects whirled around in her brain. Was one of them the man they sought, or had the killer stayed off their radar completely?

As a profiler, she'd worked a lot of serial cases and few killers managed to commit the perfect crimes. Eventually he'd make a mistake, but how many women would die before that happened?

The local media had been informed that any woman receiving long-stem roses from a secret admirer should contact Matt immediately, but what if the murderer changed things up in an effort to continue his killing spree?

Three or four days from now it would no longer be her problem. Hopefully she'd be back in Kansas City. She'd come here wanting to find justice for Miranda's murder, had doubted that the local small-town authorities would be able to get the job done.

She no longer doubted Matt and his team's abilities. With or without her help they'd eventually find the guilty party.

And eventually Matt would find love with a woman who was all the things he wanted, all the things she was not. She was surprised by how this thought sent an aching arrow of pain through her.

You told me you're not a quitter, but you're quitting on yourself. You're quitting on us.

Matt's words played in her head. He was right. And she wasn't just a quitter, she was a coward, afraid to hope that he and she could make something special, something lasting. She was fearful to allow herself to believe in anything remotely resembling happiness. She was only thirty years old and she'd already given up on herself, on life.

She remained on the bench until afternoon, when the streets grew silent and the sun bore down on her with such intensity that a headache blossomed and pounded at her skull.

Twice in the last couple of hours she'd seen one of the deputies step out of the sheriff's office and glance her way and she knew Matt had instructed them to keep an eye on her.

It was just after two when she finally gave up the bench and went into the café. The lunch crowd had all left and it was way too early for the dinner crowd to have arrived. The place was empty except for Michael who was wiping down the countertop.

"Where is everyone?" she asked as she sat on a stool in front of him.

"Sally ran home for her lunch break and I never know for sure where Leroy goes on his breaks. He took off about five minutes ago."

"I'm sure he went wherever it's cool. It's a scorcher out there today." She reached for the glass of iced water he had poured for her.

Michael frowned. "I hate it when it gets this hot. My lunch business goes down the tubes. And speaking of business, what can I get you?"

"How about a club sandwich and a glass of iced tea," Jenna said.

"Be right back." He disappeared into the kitchen area but returned almost immediately, his eyes wide. "Agent Taylor, you've got to see this," he said.

"What? What's going on?" A burst of adrenaline ripped through her as she slid off the stool and grabbed her gun from her purse.

Michael shook his head, tears filling his eyes as he

gestured for her to follow him. "I knew that boy was going to be trouble, but I had no idea how far he'd go."

Leroy! Was he the man they'd been seeking to find?

She held her gun in front of her as she trailed him through the silent kitchen and toward the backdoor.

Michael leaned weakly against the door jamb, a sick pallor on his face as he gestured her through the door.

Jenna took a step outside into the alley. All her senses were on alert as she smelled the odor of rotting fruits and vegetables coming from the nearby Dumpster, felt the heat that was rising from the asphalt, but saw nothing that might have disturbed Michael.

A tiny alarm sounded in her brain but before she could respond to it, something crashed into the back of her skull and darkness rushed up to grab her.

IT WAS DIFFICULT FOR Matt to concentrate on the files in front of him when all he could think about was Jenna. Jenna with her stubborn, independent streak, Jenna with her acerbic sense of humor and intelligence, she'd crawled into his heart and lodged herself there.

She'd spent the entire day outside, sitting on first one bench and then another and he knew she was braving the heat to avoid any contact with him.

He hadn't worried too much about her being out there alone. She'd reminded him before she left that she had a gun and she was on guard. Besides, it was daylight and there were people around. The killer wouldn't take a chance when there might be witnesses.

Had Matt gotten through to her at all? Had his words of love found purchase in her heart? Somehow he didn't think so and the thought that she would walk away from him hurt far more than he'd expected.

He wanted it all again, love and marriage and the possibility of children and he wanted it with Jenna. He wanted to begin each day with her next to him in bed and complete the day the same way.

"Sheriff, I just wanted to let you know that I don't see her on the street anywhere," Joey said from his doorway.

"She probably went in some place out of the heat," Matt replied. "Thanks, Joey."

As Joey left, Matt stared back down at the file open in front of him. It was Miranda's murder book. Had her best friend's murder forever closed the door to Jenna's heart?

He closed the file and got up from his desk as his stomach growled with hunger pangs. He hadn't had breakfast and he'd skipped lunch and if he had to guess where Jenna had gone to beat the heat, it was probably the café.

Maybe he'd just head down to the café and order a piece of Michael's pie. The sugar fix would get him through until dinner time.

Hell, who was he kidding? He wanted to check up

on Jenna and maybe, just maybe he would say something or do something that would make her realize she belonged with him forever.

He stepped out of his inner office and saw Joey and Abe at their desks. Abe was on the phone, calling floral shops, as he'd been doing for the last week.

"Maybe I'll take a walk up the street and see if I can get a glimpse of the elusive Agent Taylor," he said to Joey. "And I think I'll stop in at the café. I've been thinking about a piece of Michael's lemon pie."

Joey grinned appreciatively. "Michael does make great pies."

"His lemon is the best on the face of the earth," Matt replied.

He stepped out of the building and caught his breath as the heat slapped him in the face. Today definitely had to be the hottest day so far this summer.

He started down the sidewalk at a leisurely pace, checking the shops he passed for some sign of Jenna. It had definitely gotten too hot for her to be comfortable sitting outside.

Drat the woman anyway. She could have come into the sheriff's office if she wasn't so stubborn, if she wasn't so hard-headed. If she wasn't so wounded, a little voice whispered.

And she was wounded by a childhood of neglect, by a mother who refused to do the right thing and release her so she could truly feel loved and like she belonged.

The real question was if she was too damaged to reach out? Even if she couldn't find love with him he hoped she eventually found it with somebody else. He wanted her to love, to be loved.

He walked down Main Street one side and up the other and finally walked through the door into the cool interior of the café.

Ralph Cotter and Raymond Sinclair sat at the counter arguing about politics while Leroy stood behind it, looking harassed and irritated.

"Ralph. Raymond," Matt said as he slid onto a stool next to the two older men. "Solved the world problems yet?" The two men were both widowers and neighbors and often met for coffee and a rousing debate at the café.

"How can I fix the world when I can't even get this one fool to listen to me?" Ralph exclaimed.

"Huh, I'm not the fool around here," Raymond replied. "But there's definitely a fool sitting next to me."

Matt smiled and looked at Leroy. "Has Jenna been in?"

Leroy poured coffee for Ralph and Raymond. "Not that I know, but I just got back from my break and I don't even know where Michael is."

"I'd like to know where my burger is," Ralph said.

"It's coming, it's coming." Leroy looked at Matt. "What do you want?"

"Just a piece of pie," Matt replied.

"I've got to go turn those burgers. The pies are in

the cooler if you want to come back with me and grab the kind you want," Leroy said as he set the coffeepot down and hurried back toward the kitchen.

"Poor kid can't do more than one thing at a time," Ralph said. "I like it better when Michael's here to wait on us."

Matt got off his stool and walked around the counter and into the kitchen where Leroy stood in front of the grill. "He always yells at me when I'm a second late getting back from a break, but I got back on time a few minutes ago and the whole place was empty. Pies are on the second shelf. As far as I'm concerned you can take the whole thing with you."

It was obvious Leroy was more than irritated with his uncle as he slapped a handful of onions on the grill, their sizzle and scent filling the air.

Matt had been in the walk-in refrigerator unit a couple of times before and had always marveled at how clean and organized Michael kept it.

The pies were on a shelf, lined up in a row and marked with a sticker on the side of the pie tin. He found the lemon and slid it off the shelf and was about to leave the cooler when he saw something small and dark on the floor.

At first he thought it was a roach and his appetite instantly died. But when it didn't move, he placed the pie back on the shelf and bent down to look closer.

His heart stopped.

A petal.

A half-dried rose petal.

His thoughts shot in a hundred directions. Why would there be roses in this cooler? Who had put them in here? Michael? Leroy? Were there others? Was there a vase holding three roses intended for Jenna?

With his heart pounding, he began to search the walk-in, looking for more evidence of roses. He finally found what he sought in the very back, dark corner— a vase half-filled with water with another rose petal floating on top.

Positively electrified, he grabbed his radio from his belt. "Joey, you and Abe get over to the café and tell all the deputies to meet me here ASAP." Matt re-clipped his radio to his belt, his blood like ice flowing through his veins.

"Sheriff? Everything all right?" Leroy asked from the door of the cooler.

Matt flew at him. He grabbed him by the front of the shirt and backed him up against the wall. "Why are there rose petals in your cooler?"

"What?" Leroy's eyes were wide. "I don't know what you're talking about! You're hurting me!"

Matt let him go. The confusion, the fear in Leroy's eyes made him believe he was telling the truth. "Where's Michael?"

"I told you before, I don't know. I came back from my break and he wasn't here."

At that moment Abe and Joey came through the kitchen doors. "There's a flower vase in the back of the cooler, I want it collected and be careful, I'm hoping we'll get prints off it. Get the rest of the men to look for Jenna. It's possible she's in a store someplace or out on the street. Radio me as soon as somebody finds her."

God, he hoped that's where she was, buying something frivolous, unaware that the case was breaking wide open. "Joey, come with me. We're headed to Michael's place. I want to talk to him now." He looked at Leroy. "And you, don't leave here until we have this all sorted out."

Matt left the café with Joey at his side, a burn of fear searing through him. Michael? Was it possible that Michael was behind all of this?

He would have known both women who'd been murdered because Miranda had worked for him and Carolyn often ate lunch at the café. Good old Michael, he hadn't even been on their list of suspects.

He and Joey raced back to the office where Matt's official car was parked out front. They got in the car and took off for Michael's house.

"I can't believe it," Joey said. "I can't believe it might be Michael."

"He and Leroy would be the only people who would know what was in that walk-in and I can't imagine why Michael would have roses in there." Matt felt sick to his stomach. What he wanted more than anything at the moment was for one of his deputies to radio in and report to him that they had Jenna.

"But why? Why would he kill those women? It doesn't make any sense," Joey exclaimed.

"I'm betting there's a reason. It might not make sense to you or to me, but it will make sense to the killer in some sick, twisted way," Matt replied.

Michael Brown lived in a small ranch house on three acres of land north of town. Matt had never driven the distance so quickly.

He didn't use his siren. He didn't want to give Michael any warning that they were coming. As the neat, attractive ranch house came into view, Matt's stomach clenched with unbearable tension.

"His car isn't out front," Joey said, stating the obvious.

"That doesn't mean he's not here," Matt replied. "He could have parked it in the garage or someplace else." He pulled up front and the two of them got out.

Both of them pulled their guns and approached the front door slowly. Matt's heart was in his throat. Where was Jenna? Why hadn't anyone contacted him to let him know she'd been found?

Even though he told himself that surely Michael would never hurt her, visions of Miranda and Carolyn burst in his brain, stoking his fear for Jenna even higher.

"Michael?" he called as Joey banged on the door with his fist. The only sound was that of insects buzzing and clicking in the yard and a dog barking in the distance.

Joey knocked again and then tried the doorknob. "It's locked," he said.

"Probable cause," Matt said just before he lowered his shoulder and slammed into the door. The lock sprang and the door creaked open.

"Michael. It's Matt," he yelled as he slid through the door into the living room. Joey followed close behind him. "Michael, are you here? Come on out. I need to talk to you."

The living room was neat and clean. "Stay here and watch the front door," Matt said softly as he headed toward the kitchen. He didn't want Michael sneaking out while they checked this end of the house.

It took him only a second to see that there was nobody in the kitchen and then he joined Joey again at the front door. "We need to check out the bedrooms," he said with a sense of dread.

Please don't let me find her on the bed with a rose on her chest, he prayed as they slowly advanced down the hallway to the bedrooms.

He should have insisted she stay in the office. He should have made sure that somebody was with her at all times. Guilt nearly crippled him as he thought of all the things he should have done.

The first doorway they came to was a bathroom. As Joey covered him, Matt stepped inside and yanked back the shower curtain. A whoosh of relief escaped his lips when he saw only a gleaming white tub.

The first bedroom they came to was converted to an office with a desk and computer and shelves containing cookbooks. As Joey entered the second bedroom, he gasped and stumbled back against Matt.

Matt's heart stopped mid-beat. As he entered the room he realized they'd discovered their killer and the motive. The room was papered with copies of the same photo—one of Michael with a brown-haired, blue-eyed woman.

"I know her," Matt said as he stepped closer to the wall. "Her name was Sylvia something. She was an old college friend of Carolyn's who had spent a month visiting here in town. I didn't know she and Michael had even dated."

"This must have been the trigger," Joey said and pointed to a wedding announcement thumbtacked to the wall. The wedding between Sylvia Collins and Edward Shaw had taken place a week before the first murder. "She kind of looks like Miranda and Carolyn."

And Jenna. The words thundered in Matt's head. She'd received three roses; there should have been three left in that vase in the walk-in cooler at the café, but the vase had been empty.

Jenna had believed that he wouldn't break his ritual and that she still had three days before he'd come for her. But she'd been wrong. He prayed that she wasn't dead wrong.

"Sheriff, there's one more bedroom," Joey said.

Matt's heart pounded so loud that he barely heard the deputy's voice. His knees felt weak and for the first time in his career he thought he might throw up.

He reached inside for strength and with a nod to Joey they stepped back out into the hallway and toward the closed master bedroom door.

As Joey kept his gun leveled in front of him, Matt gripped the knob and flung open the door. He nearly collapsed to his knees as he saw the bed, neatly made with a brown comforter and nothing else.

No Jenna.

No roses.

His relief was short-lived. She was out there somewhere and so was Michael—with three roses and the need to kill.

Chapter Twelve

Roses.

She smelled the lush unmistakable scent of roses.
A tiny alarm went off in the back of Jenna's brain, but
as she cracked open her eyes and saw her surround-
ings, the alarm faded and she relaxed.

She was safe in Matt's bedroom, in his bed. She'd
had the craziest dream—no, it had definitely been a
nightmare. It was only when she tried to turn to see
Matt next to her that sudden sheer panic set in.

She couldn't turn over. Her wrists were tied to the
headboard and something covered her mouth. Any
thought that this was a dream shot away as memories
spilled into her head.

The café.

Michael.

She remembered following him through the
kitchen, then stepping out the backdoor, then nothing.

Although at the moment she was in the room alone,

she knew she was in trouble. Roses lay on the mattress on either side of her. Four and five, she thought. And the sixth was the rose of death.

She yanked at the rope that held her wrists, sheer terror coursing through her. Dear God, nobody knew she was here. Nobody knew it was Michael. She had no idea where he was at the moment but knew that sooner or later he'd come back into the room to deliver the sixth and final rose to her.

A sob rose up inside her as she twisted and pulled at the ropes, but there was no give. She'd thought she had time. She'd believed she'd see him coming, but she'd been wrong, so wrong.

Where was Matt now? Sitting in his office? Chatting with his deputies? Unaware that she was in danger? Not knowing that Michael was the killer they sought?

Suddenly her fear of loving Matt seemed ridiculous and childish. He'd been right. Everything he'd said to her was right. She loved him and she wanted everything she knew loving him would bring into her life.

And now it was all too late. She'd be nothing more than the next file on his desk, the next collection of grisly crime scene photos.

She began to pull once again on the rope that bound her wrists as new sobs racked her body. She tried to still the sobs, knowing that if her nose clogged up she'd suffocate.

"You can't get loose." The deep familiar voice

caused her to freeze. She watched through narrowed eyes as Michael came into the room. In one hand he carried the final rose and in the other the knife she knew would take her life.

No hope.

She'd never had any hope and that certainly didn't change now. There was nothing inside her but a hollow despair. She was going to die here, in the very same bed where she'd found love.

"I had to change things," Michael said, his voice a hoarse whisper. He remained standing just inside the door. "I couldn't wait to give you your roses the way they were supposed to be given."

She said his name against the tape across her mouth, but it came out as nothing but a garbled grunt. He took a step toward her and she tensed.

"You're probably wondering about all this. She was everything I ever wanted." His features took on a softness. "She was a friend of Carolyn who had come to visit for a month. Every day she'd come into the café and sit and talk with me. She had the softest brown hair and blue eyes that made me feel so special when she looked at me, when she smiled at me."

He stared at the wall just over Jenna's head, as if lost in memories. "It took me two weeks to finally work up enough nerve to ask her out and when she agreed to the date, I felt as if my life was finally complete."

He raised the rose to his nose and smelled it and a

spasm of pain raced across his face. "On that first date I brought her a rose, a token of my love for her. The next night we went out again and I brought her another rose and that night we made love. I knew she was the one who would make me whole, the one who would share my life. Five nights in a row we were together, laughing and loving and I've never been so happy in my life."

As he talked, Jenna continued to tug at the ropes. Her legs were free and she tensed them, prepared to kick if and when he got close enough.

"It was on our sixth date that everything fell apart." Thick emotion deepened his voice. "She told me she'd gotten a call from the boyfriend she'd dated before coming here, that he'd told her he missed her and he loved her, and she loved him."

A dark rage shone from his eyes and his entire body seemed to vibrate with his barely suppressed emotions. "She told me she'd had fun with me, we'd had a good time, but she didn't love me. The next day she left town. She used me," he yelled. "I was playing forever and she was playing for fun."

Jenna wanted to scream, she wanted to ask what all that had to do with her? But she knew. She knew that somehow they all had morphed into Sylvia in Michael's mind. Each time he plunged that knife into some woman's heart he was killing Sylvia for not loving him, for abandoning him.

"You're just like her," he said as he laid the final

rose on the top of Matt's dresser. "You're all just like her with your soft brown hair and innocent blue eyes. I watched Miranda flirting with the men, playing with their emotions. And Carolyn, even though she had a boyfriend, when she'd come in for lunch I saw her looking around at the other men."

He came closer to the bed, the afternoon sunshine shimmering on the blade of his knife. "And you. I see the way Matt looks at you. He's crazy about you, but you're nothing but a love-'em-and-leave-'em type. You'd have broken his heart just like she broke mine."

Jenna felt his rage building. It stole the oxygen from the room, made it difficult for her to draw a breath. She saw it in his eyes and knew the end was coming.

"WHERE COULD HE BE? Where could he have taken her?" Matt said aloud as he drove toward the café.

"Maybe Leroy knows more than he's saying," Joey replied.

"Maybe." Matt clenched the steering wheel as his brain filtered through the other crime scenes, through everything he knew about Michael Brown. Where would Michael take his next victim?

He had to face the fact that Michael had Jenna. Nobody had seen her since Michael disappeared from the café. He had to work on the assumption that she was in mortal danger and he prayed it wasn't already too late for her.

"Beds," he said suddenly.

"What?" Joey looked at him in confusion.

"He's killed both the other victims in their own beds."

"But Agent Taylor doesn't have a house here in town, she doesn't have a bed anywhere," Joey replied.

Matt grabbed his radio. "Abe, get a couple of the men to check out the motel, unit seven. Approach with caution. We're looking for Michael Brown and we can assume he's armed and dangerous." Matt dropped the radio and stepped on the gas. "And we're going to Miranda's place. Jenna owns it now. Michael might consider it Jenna's place and that's where he left the first three roses."

His heart thrummed a rhythm of panic and he remembered the last time he'd felt this way. It had been in the moments after he'd received the call that a gunman was holed up in the social services offices with hostages.

The scar on his cheek itched and burned and he fought the impulse to tear into it with his fingers. He couldn't do this again. He couldn't live through this again. She had to be all right. Jenna had to be okay.

Seconds had never felt so long, each minute an agony as he raced to Miranda's house. Thankfully Joey didn't speak because Matt didn't want to waste his energy talking.

Michael. How many times had the man smiled at him, served him food and shot the breeze and never had Matt caught a glimpse into the darkness that must reside in the man.

How had he missed it? How had Jenna missed it? He knew the answer, Michael had been smart, cunning and he hadn't made any mistakes until now.

Matt's blood froze as he thought what might have happened if he hadn't gone into the walk-in refrigerator, if he hadn't noticed that single rose petal on the floor. How many more bodies would he be dealing with if he hadn't wanted a piece of pie?

There was only one body he cared about now. Jenna. His heart cried her name as he wheeled to a halt in front of Miranda's house.

Once again he and Joey advanced cautiously on the place, their guns at the ready. The door was locked and this time it was Joey who put his shoulder to the wood and managed to get the door open.

They went in and Matt immediately bee-lined to the bedroom where he knew Jenna had slept while she'd been in the house. The room was empty. He headed toward the master bedroom, the place where Miranda had lost her life. That room was empty as well, and it didn't look as if anyone had been inside.

Think. Think! A voice cried in his head. Where could he be? Where would he have taken her? A horrifying emptiness filled him.

Too much time had gone by. It was probably already too late. No, he couldn't think that way. He had to have hope. He had to find her. Somehow he had to figure this out.

His radio crackled and Abe's voice came over the line. "Motel room is empty. Doesn't look like anyone's been in here at all."

"Thanks, Abe, keep looking for her," Matt replied.

"Where do we go from here?" Joey asked.

Matt's mind raced. He killed them in their beds. They'd checked the beds where Jenna had slept while she'd been in town.

Except yours.

The words thundered inside his brain. Was it possible? While he and his deputies had been running all over town, was Michael bold enough to take Jenna to Matt's house? To his bed?

He grabbed Joey by the arm. "My place. Let's go."

As he ran out of Miranda's house Joey was right behind him. It was at that moment that Matt recognized the killing rage building inside of him.

If Michael had hurt Jenna, then he'd never see a trial, he'd never spend a day in prison. Matt would save the judicial system the trouble of a trial. Sheriff or not, Matt was first a man and he would make sure that Michael Brown paid for Jenna's death with his own life.

The tension that filled the car as he raced to his house was nearly suffocating. "Call the men, tell them to meet us there," he directed Joey.

Joey made the call and by that time they were on Matt's street. He pulled to the curb half a block from his house and cut the engine.

"I want us to go in quietly," he said as they got out of the car. Even though he had no evidence to confirm that Michael had brought Jenna here, his gut instinct told him this was the right place. He just prayed they weren't too late.

As he gazed down the block he spied Michael's car and the alarms that rang in his head momentarily deafened him. He could only guess that Michael had pulled into his driveway, somehow unloaded Jenna and then parked up the block from the house.

Matt's neighbors, an older couple who rarely ventured outside and a younger couple, who both worked, probably wouldn't have seen anything.

As he and Joey advanced on the house Matt once again prayed they weren't too late, that Michael hadn't already killed the woman he loved.

The front door was locked and as Matt grabbed his keys, his fingers shook slightly. As quietly as possible, he unlocked the door and shoved it open.

Silence greeted him, but the hairs on the nape of his neck prickled. He motioned for Joey to follow him as he crept directly to the staircase.

When he reached the third step he heard it—the muffled sound of a male voice coming from the master bedroom, confirming that Michael was here.

What he desperately wanted to hear, what he didn't hear was any sound that would indicate that Jenna was still alive.

The master bedroom door was closed and he motioned Joey to stand on one side while he stood on the other. Matt drew a deep, steadying breath as his fingers gripped the doorknob.

In one fluid movement he turned the knob, opened the door and crashed inside. He instantly took in the horrifying scene before him.

Jenna tied to the bed, her eyes wide with fear and a rose on her chest. Michael standing at the side of the bed, a knife held high over his head.

"Halt!" Matt cried. "Put the knife down. Michael, drop the knife," he ordered. "Drop the damn knife."

Michael didn't move. "She's just like all the others," he said. "She deserves to die."

His entire body tensed and the knife raised an increment higher. Matt fired his gun. The bullet caught Michael in his side, just beneath his armpit. He froze and turned to stare at Matt, then smiled and slammed the knife down and into Jenna.

"No!" Matt screamed. He shot Michael again…and again and finally the man slumped to the floor at the side of the bed.

Matt raced to Jenna's side, deep sobs escaping him as he saw the knife in her flesh, the blood that had begun to seep from the wound. Her eyes fluttered and her skin bleached white.

He yanked the tape from her mouth. "It's going to be all right. Stay with me, Jenna," he said, vaguely aware of Joey calling for an ambulance. He knew better than to try to remove the knife from her, knew that he could cause more damage by attempting to pull it out.

With tears trekking down his cheeks, he fumbled to untie her arms, refusing to believe that this was the end, that Michael had won.

"Matt?" Her voice was reed thin and she gasped for air. "I guess I lost the bet."

Freeing both her hands, he grabbed them in his and squeezed tightly. "Hang on, Jenna. Help is on the way, just hang on."

"Please, get that damned rose off my chest," she whispered and then her eyes closed.

Matt threw the rose across the room and then grabbed her hands once again. He squeezed her fingers with his, a sob escaping him. "Jenna, wake up. Damn it, don't you be a quitter. Don't you quit on me. Wake up!"

He closed his eyes and willed her to be okay, as if by his sheer mental power alone he could keep her alive. Everything else in the room faded away as he concentrated only on her.

"Sheriff, you need to back away," Joey said. "They need to get her to the hospital."

Matt realized the paramedics had arrived. He backed

away from her and watched as they loaded her on a gurney. His grief nearly crippled him. Too late. He'd been too late.

Maybe she'd been right all along. Maybe he was the fool to hope that he could find happiness again. Maybe he was only deceiving himself in believing in happy endings.

SHE DREAMED OF MIRANDA and in the dream Miranda was lecturing her about love, about life. Miranda was the only one who Jenna had ever listened to, the only one who had ever been able to get through Jenna's thick skull.

Miranda's face morphed into her mother's and Jenna was filled with an overwhelming sadness. She couldn't go back and fix what had been broken in her mother. She hadn't been able to love her enough to slice through whatever mental problems her mother had had to find a nurturing parent.

The sadness wasn't for Jenna herself, but rather for the woman who had died alone in prison, the woman who had never known happiness or real love.

Had Jenna become the same kind of woman her mother had been? A woman incapable of reaching out for happiness? For love?

I don't want to be like you. The words thundered in her brain and she woke up. For a moment she was disoriented as she stared around the room. Her heart constricted as her gaze landed on Matt, slumped in a chair, his hair sticking up in all directions and his clothes wrinkled.

"Am I dead?" Her voice sounded rusty to her own ears.

Matt's eyes snapped open and he jumped out of the chair and was at her side. "Why would you ask?"

"Because you look like death warmed over and if I'm here with you, then I must be dead."

He smiled. The gesture began at the corner of his lips and spread across his face, softening the tension and warming his eyes. "You'd look like death, too, if you'd spent the night in that chair. Heaven wasn't quite ready for you and the devil didn't want you, so I guess you're alive."

She reached up and touched her chest, where she felt a bandage. "What's the damage?"

"He punctured your lung and did a little muscle damage, but the doctor managed to fix it all." The tension swept back on his features and his beautiful gray eyes darkened. "I thought he'd killed you. I thought I'd been too late."

"Michael?" she asked.

"Is dead. He won't hurt any more women."

Jenna closed her eyes, for a moment reliving that terrifying time just before Matt crashed through the door. "I can't believe we missed him. I can't believe he managed to fly under our radar." She opened her eyes and looked at Matt once again. "He fits the profile, but I was so focused on the others, I didn't even think about him."

"Don't beat yourself up. I was there right along with you. Michael never entered my mind as a potential suspect." He took a step back from her bed. "The good news is that the case is solved. It's finally over and I guess you can get back to your life in Kansas City knowing that Miranda's murderer is dead."

His voice was flat, empty and Jenna knew this was a defining moment in her life. She could either continue on her path to nowhere or take a chance and reach out for love with Matt.

"Actually, I've been thinking about that," she began.

He crooked a dark eyebrow. "When? While you were unconscious?"

"It's amazing how much you can think when you're tied up to a bed and believe that death is imminent." She raised the head of her bed and then continued. "While Michael was ranting and raving about the woman who had destroyed his world, all I could think about was how much I didn't want to let my mother win. How much I didn't want to spend the rest of my life without hope, without dreams and most important of all, without love."

She saw the light that shot into his eyes as he stepped closer to her. "So what exactly do you intend to do about it?"

"I'm always going to be stubborn, Matt. And there's a part of me that's still just a little bit afraid."

"I've been known to be a little stubborn myself," he replied. "And believe me, Jenna. There's nothing to be afraid of."

Looking into the dove-gray softness of his eyes, she believed him. "I still have a lot of work to do at Miranda's house and I was thinking maybe I'd put in for a transfer to the Dallas field office," she said.

Matt said nothing, he simply continued to gaze at her and she knew he was waiting for her to say the words, waiting for her to begin their future.

He would take good care of her love. She had no doubt where that was concerned. He would cherish her and together they would build the kind of life she'd never dreamed possible.

"I told you once that I had no hopes, no dreams," she said. "But when I look into your eyes so many dreams unfold in my head, so many hopes fill my heart. I love you, Matt, and I want to stick around and have all those things realized with you."

He closed his eyes for a long moment and when he opened them again the happiness that shone there nearly stole her breath away.

He leaned down and kissed her cheek. "You'll never be sorry, Jenna. I'm your partner, your lover and we're going to spend the rest of our lives building our dreams."

Our dreams. The words shimmered inside Jenna's heart and she knew she'd finally found the place where she belonged.

Epilogue

It had been three weeks since Michael Brown had been shot to death and Jenna had declared her love for Matt. Once again Matt had found himself heralded as a hero. The mayor had given him a bronze plaque, but the real trophy Matt had gained at the moment had her butt up in the air as she packed the last large box of Miranda's clothing to give to charity.

"Are you staring at my butt?" Her voice was muffled inside the box.

"I am, and it's a fine butt," he said with a grin.

She straightened and grinned at him. "If you really cared, you'd carry this box outside for me."

"If you really cared, you'd come over here and give me a kiss," he replied.

"I'm always up for that, Sheriff Buchannan."

As she walked toward him, Matt felt the familiar excitement, the sizzle of desire that he knew he'd always feel for her.

In the past three weeks his love for her had only grown stronger and he knew she felt the same way about him. She'd opened up herself, gifted him with seeing inside her heart and had become a loving, giving woman.

She slid into his awaiting arms and raised her face to look up at him. "Just one," she said. "You know Sam is supposed to meet us here any minute."

Sam Connelly, Jenna's fellow FBI agent and friend, had agreed to drive down and bring Jenna her cat, Whiskers. Sam was at the beginning of a two-week vacation.

"Just one," Matt agreed and took her mouth with his. As always, a simple kiss with Jenna took only a taste to become something hot and wild and wonderful.

It was magic, having her in his arms, tasting her mouth with his and he knew that magic would last as long as they both lived.

As the kiss deepened she wrapped her arms around his neck and molded herself to him, fitting like the missing piece of the puzzle that had been his life.

"Hmm."

The sound of a throat clearing jerked them apart. Matt turned to see a dark-haired, blue-eyed man standing in the doorway holding a cat carrier.

"Sam!" Jenna exclaimed. "It's so good to see you." She quickly made the introductions between the two men. Matt instantly liked Sam. Maybe it was because he knew Jenna trusted and respected the man and maybe it was because he knew there had never been any romantic sparks between the two.

"I'm glad to see that a little thing like a serial killer can't get the best of you," Sam said to Jenna.

"I realized I had too much to live for," she replied and reached for Matt's hand.

"I heard you put in for a transfer." Sam set the cat carrier on the floor next to him.

"I'm on medical leave for another couple of weeks and I'm hoping by then the transfer will be approved," she explained. She pulled Matt forward. "Matt, you need to meet my cat." She forced him to lean down to greet the cat who hissed and snarled.

"I can tell she's related to you," Matt said drily.

Sam released a burst of laughter as Jenna punched him in the arm. "Ah, it looks like you've finally met your match, Jenna," he said with a conspiratorial wink at Matt.

Jenna tilted her head and looked at Sam with affection. "Someday, I hope you meet your match, Sam."

"Not me," he replied. "Remember, I'm the prince of darkness and I have yet to meet a woman who can light my path out of the dark." He pulled a set of keys out of his pocket. "And now, I'm off."

"So soon? Jenna thought you might want to stay at our place, at least for the night," Matt said.

Sam shook his head. "Thanks for the offer, but I'm eager to get to my vacation spot, a nice quiet bed and breakfast in Bachelor Moon, Louisiana."

"Thanks for taking care of Whiskers for me," Jenna said as they walked Sam to the front door.

"That cat has issues," he replied.

Matt grinned. "I know all about women with issues."

Sam returned his smile. "You two have a great life," he said as he stepped out of the door.

"You, too, Sam," Jenna said and leaned into Matt as they walked the tall, good-looking agent to his car in the driveway.

It was only after his car had disappeared from sight that Matt pulled her back into his arms. "Now, where were we before we were so rudely interrupted?" he asked.

She smiled up at him, her blue eyes shimmering with happiness. "I think we were right here," she said and raised up on her tiptoes to press her lips against his.

Matt intended to spend every day for the rest of his life loving Jenna, showing her how precious she was to him, how important she was in his life.

When the kiss ended she placed a hand on his face, warming the scar that had once ripped into his soul. "I love you, Matt."

"And I love you," he replied. "Let's get out of here."

"Yes, it's time to truly say goodbye to Miranda." She

picked up the painting that had hung in the entryway of the house, the painting she'd told him she'd once given to her friend.

"I'm ready," Jenna said and smiled and in the warmth of her eyes he saw not only his own dreams, but hers as well, shining bright like their future together.

* * * * *

*Bestselling author Lynne Graham is back
with a fabulous new trilogy!*

PREGNANT BRIDES

Three ordinary girls—naive, but also honest and plucky…

*Three fabulously wealthy, impossibly handsome
and very ruthless men…*

*When opposites attract and passion leads to pregnancy…
it can only mean marriage!*

*Available next month from Harlequin Presents®:
the first installment*

DESERT PRINCE, BRIDE OF INNOCENCE

* * *

'THIS EVENING I'm flying to New York for two weeks,' Jasim imparted with a casualness that made her heart sink like a stone. 'That's why I had you brought here. I own this apartment and you'll be comfortable here while I'm abroad.'

'I can afford my own accommodation although I may not need it for long. I'll have another job by the time you get back—'

Jasim released a slightly harsh laugh. 'There's no need for you to look for another position. How would I ever see you? Don't you understand what I'm offering you?'

Elinor stood very still. 'No, I must be incredibly thick because I haven't quite worked out yet what you're offering me….'

His charismatic smile slashed his lean dark visage. 'Naturally, I want to take care of you….'

'No, thanks.' Elinor forced a smile and mentally willed him not to demean her with some sordid proposition. 'The only man who will ever take *care* of me with my agreement will be my husband. I'm willing to wait for you to come back but I'm not willing to be kept by you. I'm a very independent woman and what I give, I give freely.'

Jasim frowned. 'You make it all sound so serious.'

'What happened between us last night left pure chaos in its wake. Right now, I don't know whether I'm on my head or my heels. I'll stay for a while because I have nowhere else to go in the short term. So maybe it's good that you'll be away for a while.'

Jasim pulled out his wallet to extract a card. 'My private number,' he told her, presenting her with it as though it was a precious gift, which indeed it was. Many women would have done just about anything to gain access to that direct hotline to him, but his staff guarded his privacy with scrupulous care.

Before he could close the wallet, his blood ran cold in his veins. How could he have made such a serious oversight? What if he had got her pregnant? He knew that an unplanned pregnancy would engulf his life like an avalanche, crush his freedom and suffocate him. He barely stilled a shudder at the threat of such an outcome and thought how ironic it was that what his older brother had longed and prayed for to secure the line to the throne should strike Jasim as an absolute disaster....

* * *

What will proud Prince Jasim do if Elinor is expecting his royal baby? Perhaps an arranged marriage is the only solution! But will Elinor agree? Find out in DESERT PRINCE, BRIDE OF INNOCENCE by Lynne Graham [#2884], available from Harlequin Presents® in January 2010.

HPEX0110B

HARLEQUIN *Presents*

Bestselling Harlequin Presents author

Lynne Graham

brings you an exciting new miniseries:

PREGNANT BRIDES

Inexperienced and expecting, they're forced to marry

Collect them all:

DESERT PRINCE, BRIDE OF INNOCENCE

January 2010

RUTHLESS MAGNATE, CONVENIENT WIFE

February 2010

GREEK TYCOON, INEXPERIENCED MISTRESS

March 2010

REQUEST YOUR FREE BOOKS!

2 FREE NOVELS
PLUS 2
FREE GIFTS!

◆ HARLEQUIN®

INTRIGUE®

Breathtaking Romantic Suspense

HI09R

New Year, New Man!

*For the perfect New Year's punch,
blend the following:*

- *One woman determined to find her inner vixen*
- *A notorious—and notoriously hot!—playboy*
- *A provocative New Year's Eve bash*
- *An impulsive kiss that leads to a night of
explosive passion!*

When the clock hits midnight Claire Daniels
kisses the guy standing closest to her, but
the kiss doesn't end after the bells stop ringing....

Look for

Moonstruck

by *USA TODAY* bestselling author

JULIE KENNER

Available January

---

red-hot reads

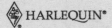